ISBN: 978-1-4709-4116-1

www.jakezuurbier.com

The detective

Jake Zuurbier

Table Of Contents

The Detective
By Michael Davis

hapter one

"I wrote," I said. "Swear to god, I just finished writing."

"Really?" The guy said sarcastically. "And how far along are you?"

"Far enough," I replied.

"Mike, if you don't meet quota, you—," he scoffed. "I can't do shit if you don't finish in time even if I wanted to." I leaned my head against the wall behind me. I knew he couldn't.

"I know," I said.

"And I know you haven't been feeling this one, but you can't give up on it like you did the last few ideas. Time is money and you're wasting theirs— ours, I mean."

"It's just a subjectively bad story."

"Brother, objectively. You're the object. It's not bad. Come on man," the guy replied. I closed my eyes and pinched the bridge of my nose.

"Michael," he went on.

"Don't call me that."

"Don't call your work bad."

"Tell them I'll have it done, nothing to worry about." I looked at the ceiling, at my red lamp. A souvenir from Jessica.

"Mike, I love you, I really do, but you're the *only* thing I worry about." I put the phone on speaker and flipped mindlessly trough a photography magazine.

"Quite a boring life, then," I said, stopping to look at a picture of a woman dancing in a red dress. Flamingo? Flamenco? Flaming hot.

I could almost taste the hopeless moment of silence the guy at the other side of the phone brought into the room. I sighed and threw down the magazine.

"I'll pull something out of my ass."
"You better pull quick."
"Yeah, yeah. You've got my word. Say hi to them from me."
"Your word doesn't mean anything to them, if you don't deliver at least a first draft of the full story they'll fire you, man," the guy said.
"I know, and I will." It was silent for a few seconds.
"How are you, anyway?" He asked.
"I'm alright," I said.
"That's good, that's good." I nodded though I knew no one could see.
"You think you can deliver the first draft by next week?" He asked. Fuck no.
"Yeah, sure. It's basically done, I just need to add an end to it."
"As long as it's just an end, not a middle and a start too." The beeping of my phone signaled the conversation was over.

My publishers office was a bit of a pain in the ass lately. Nothing new, they told me to work and I didn't. I used to pump out books like a gold-shitting donkey when I first started working with them, most of them getting successful right away. I was over a decade younger then, I don't have the same inspiration anymore.
You know how it goes, I set a standard back then and I can't reach it anymore. Don't have the same inspiration or motivation. When donkeys get nothing to eat, can you really expect them to be pushing out logs of gold every day? No, they fucking die.

2

I can't find an ending because the story doesn't make any fucking sense. I started without a plot, didn't even know the killer. Still don't. I started really stretching the scenes out really quickly just to fill the page count. I wasn't lying about having a beginning and a middle part, it was right there in front of me, in the opened document on my laptop. The letters on it mocked me, the last date of edit over three weeks ago. I slammed it shut and threw it besides the magazine on the small table. I won't lie, I hadn't read it for a few weeks.

I swung my legs on the desk and stared out of the window in front of it. I just sat there, not doing anything. Paralyzed, almost frozen. I didn't want to keep writing. It felt like I'd just hit a dead end, pun intended. It being a murder mystery and all, if you catch my train of thought. This shit always happened when I tried to make money off of things. It would just feel useless and I almost always lost interest real quick. I wasn't against making money, because I was doing that for a while already. My brain just didn't want to keep doing that shit. It didn't find it fun anymore.

My head fell to the right, neck muscles just not bothering anymore. I stared out into the night. Didn't see a single star, it seemed semi light out even when it was night around here. Light pollution.

I put up a middle finger to my laptop and plopped down on my couch. My cat brushed against the doorpost and walked into the room.
"So you're still alive," I said. The cat let out a meow of acknowledgement.

"As you can see, so am I," I continued. "You'll have food for yet another day." The cat walked up to me and started brushing against my leg.

"Not now though, wanker, it's the middle of the night. Are you crazy?" The cat started purring. Power move, he learned I couldn't resist if he did that shit.

"Hustler. Fine, come on. Let's get you a midnight snack," I said and stood up.

I closed my eyes for a second against the lightheadedness and started walking, relying fully on my other senses. My hands, mainly. My vision quickly came back, luckily. There might've been no stars outside but I had some in my eye sockets every time I stood up.

"You feel like meat or nah?" I asked the tiny beast. I shuffled towards the kitchen and opened up some cabinets. The cat meowed loudly and did a little jump to show his clear anticipation.

"Calm down dude, don't be too eager." I took the box of cat food out of the cabinet and shook it. No sound. I frowned like an idiot and looked inside it. No food.

"Guess I was wrong. I'm alive but you get *no* food." I sighed loudly and the cat seemed to sigh a just as dramatic sigh. Metaphorically, all he did was meow very angrily.

"Dude, it's fate. The universe doesn't want you getting fat. Take that sign. I'll get food tomorrow." I threw the empty box in the direction of the trashcan. I missed, but the cat jumped straight to it.

"There's no — never mind, good luck."

I sat my ass back on the couch and put on the tv. I didn't even like tv, I just put it on for the sound. Like a background sound for my thoughts. Or lack thereof. The red bottle of vodka on the ground next to me caught my attention. It matched my red lamp. I tilted my head and kept my gaze on it. It was half empty already, didn't remember how it got like that. I could guess, though. Probably drank it. Wouldn't have been the cat, he'd be dead.

"Do you feel like life has slowed down?" A voice on the tv said. My gaze got sucked to the ad.
"Blow new life into your sex life with OtherLove dot com. Consensual adventure!"
"Consensual cheating," I mumbled. I grabbed the bottle of vodka and put it to my mouth. I hesitated, but that moment passed almost immediately. The burn ran down my throat and into my stomach. I barely even felt it anymore, it was like when you're lactose intolerant but keep eating cheese, you'll eventually get used to the pain.

It was a bottle with a handle, I tried balancing the handle on two fingers. It felt pretty fucking pointless. Not it, to be fair. I. I didn't feel like I did anything anymore. I was just there. I was moving but I wasn't making any movements forward. Not even backwards, though the writers block wasn't something I was happy with.

I chugged another double-shot worth of vodka. I heard my cat still attacking the food box. Wasn't any use as far as I could hear, but respect for the effort. Without much effort I put my head on the couch and closed my eyes. I could barely feel a buzz coming in. I took another sip of the vodka and with a limp arm let it rest beside me on the couch.

Out of breath I woke up and tried sitting up. The cat fell off of my face into my lap and put his claws in me.

5

"Fuck!" I yelled, sprung up and instinctively grabbed my legs, dropping something on the ground that used to be in my hand. Glass shattered and spread across the entire floor. The cat jumped back up on the couch and hissed. "Motherfucker," I let out and rubbed my legs. "Piece of shit, fuck." I turned around to the cat.

"Didn't mean that. God damn does it hurt though." Only a little bit of blood came from the scratches the cat made. I sighed and looked at the pieces of glass. It was impressive how much small pieces came from just one bottle. The floor was filled with tiny red shards. No alcohol, I probably drank it all. The light from the window reflected in the pieces of glass, making the entire room shimmer red. A bit like a slasher or some shit. Looked like blood was dripping from the walls.

I stood there for a couple of minutes, procrastinating the cleanup. My cat yelled at me, which was fair. I would yell if I almost got killed by a bottle. I yelled when he put his nails in me, so I got it.

"Why the fuck were you on my face dude?"

My feet brushed the sidewalk as I walked past prospect park. I didn't usually walk to the store. To be honest, I didn't go there that much at all. I usually just ordered online. Figured I might as well today, it was early and I felt weirdly motivated. Might've been the alcohol still in my system, but it was a while since I felt any at all. Was cheaper than ordering online too. Online service is a blessing and a curse all in one. Hadn't talked to someone in person for a long, long time, aside from delivery boys. Most people I talked to was over the phone or via face calls. The last one I saw might've been my ex when I dropped her shit off at her place. Was a couple months ago. Jesus, I'd become a hermit.

The leaves on the sidewalk stuck to my shoes. There weren't that many people around, which wasn't surprising for the time of day. The store had probably barely opened, the sun was barely up. It was the first time in a while that I was awake at this time. Hadn't seen the sun come up in even longer than when I saw my ex. The sunrise was nice, but it was cold. I hated fall. Couldn't wait until spring started. Lost in thought I walked on, almost hypnotized by the cars that passed by.

"Watch where you're going, mate," I heard and looked up. I almost walked into this dude with his girlfriend. His coat was one of those wool ones that are so unnecessarily long they reach your knees. Big coat to make up for something else. His girl had blond hair, it was dancing in the wind. It was put up in a ponytail, a high one. My head jerked as I looked back at them.
"Jessica!" I said, more out of surprise than anything else. Fucking hell, the last thing I wanted was to talk to her. Why the hell did I do that? I turned back around as quick as I could, hoping she didn't hear. To my horror I heard her turn around, two coats rustling against each other. I kept walking. I wasn't in the mood for whatever the fuck they had going on.

"Mike!" I heard. Footsteps came running after me. I felt a soft hand grab my arm, stopping me from walking away. It didn't work, I kept walking.
"Is that you?"
I turned to her, faking a smile. Didn't stop walking, hoping she would get the hint. She didn't.
"Hey, how've you been?" She asked.
"As you would expect," I said. Jason caught up to us, looking just as happy as I did.

"Michael," he said with a short nod, then turned to Jess. "We need to go, honey. We can't be late." He put his hand on her shoulder and nodded his head towards wherever they were going.

"I'm sure they can wait one minute," she said. I didn't hate them, I just strongly disliked them. Especially Jason, he's the kinda guy that gets everything handed to him.

"Yes, they could, but why would we let them?" he said.

"Sounds important, think you shouldn't let them wait," I said. I dodged Jessica's gaze, instead stared at the reflective windows of a building on the other side of the street. Her blue eyes pierced my soul even though I didn't look directly at them.

"How is your book coming along?" she asked, like she didn't hear either of us. I couldn't tell if she was genuinely curious or mocking me. She probably knew I hit a writer's block by lack of, frankly, her.

I stopped walking, causing Jason to walk into me. He sent me a pissed look. I couldn't care less.

"It's alright," I just said. I didn't feel like talking to her, especially about my book.

"Let me know when it's done," Jess continued. Definitely mocking me.

"Sure," I replied sarcastically.

"I'm sure your life is exhilarating and I would love to stay and chat, mate, but we've got somewhere to be," Jason said and gently guided Jessica in the direction they were first going.

"How's life with a tiny dick?" I asked Jason, after which I turned away and started walking away from both them and wherever it was they were going.

"Seems to me like it's preferred over yours," Jason said. I heard them walking away. Fucking asshole.

I don't know when I came home. I just came in, poured the cat a bowl of food and now sat on the couch with another bottle of vodka. It was half empty. Or full, depending on how you look at it. Drunk no matter which. I wasn't sobered up from last night, but at least I wouldn't be hungover today. Can't be when you're constantly drunk. Fucking pathetic.

The bottle felt cold in my hand, the rounding of the glass uneven. I couldn't see it that well. Maybe because my room was dark, maybe because I was half a bottle of vodka away from a night in the hospital with a pump in my stomach. I took another sip. Glad I mixed vodka with vodka though, could've been worse if I mixed it with another type of alcohol.

I noticed my laptop as I put the bottle of vodka beside me on the floor. I stared at it for a good five minutes, trying to focus my blurry vision.
"You're a bitch," I then told it. I stood up, turned the TV on and grabbed the bottle of vodka.
"You want one?" I asked my cat who walked into the room. I scoffed and shook my head. I continued in my silly cat voice, the one I only use on my cat when no one's around.
"You don't even know what work is, do you? You don't have to work for your food."
The cap of the vodka bottle disappeared into the trash and I grabbed my laptop. As I walked to the dinner table I chugged over a shot's worth of alcohol.
"And the worst thing is that I'm jealous," I said to the cat. I put the laptop down on the table and stared at it again, like it'd start throwing words at me, telling me what the hell to write. I sat down on the chair and looked back at the cat, now licking himself.

9

"I want to just *get* food without working for it." I chugged another shot of vodka that tasted like nothing.
"And lick my ass in public."

Slowly I started scrolling up, seeing the chapters fly by faster every time I scrolled. The brightness of the screen was rough in contrast with the darkness from outside. Probably night. Another sip.
This story sucked. I still didn't know who killed the old rich guy even though I was the one writing. I couldn't decide between the long lost relative and the rich asshole. Imagine if the rich asshole did it, he'd be sent to die in jail. That'd be a happy ending for everyone.

That asshole took my girl, he showed up to her tours in the museum and they'd fuck in front of mona lisa or Leo DaVinci or whoever. That son of a bitch explored her hidden tomb.
I took another sip as the words rolled down the screen. Jessica was even worse, she was the one in a relationship, the one who actually did the cheating. God, Jessica. A half-cry left my throat, but right after, an embarrassed cough came out to restore the shrivel that was still left of my dignity. I met her at a party. I was just as drunk as I was now, if not drunker. My alcohol tolerance was higher now, but it was far from low back then. I barely could even see her face in the flashing, colored lights, but I immediately knew she was hot. She was, I wasn't wrong about that, but she was like a succubus. Amazing sex but makes you slowly die the longer you go on.

I rubbed my eyes with both my hands but it didn't make it any less blurry. If anything, I fucked my vision up more for a couple seconds. I stopped scrolling and stared at the screen intently with a slanted jaw, trying to concentrate.

10

"Joan and Jack stood in the living room of the mansion, waiting for the count to reappear to make his announcement," I read out loud. Joan and Jack, Jessica and Jason. I felt inspired with the J names, clearly. They were a pair of bitches. I shouldn't have put them in my story, probably didn't help with the productivity level. I didn't want to see them in real life, what made me think I wanted to see them on my screen? Even for the sake of fake revenge.

There is nothing *wrong* with detective novels, they're good books usually. The writers who wrote them had a good thing going, even if there was a formula. Good plot and characters. Writing them is the part that always gets me. Look, I don't hate the idea of a parody. Parodies are great. I just hate the way I *personally* wrote it. I scrolled further up.

"Nancy was preparing the drinks, every single one differently, since none of the guests had the same drink. She hurried off to the bathroom." I could barely make out the letters anymore. I liked Nancy, though I had done what other writers had done too, made her the screaming maid. Was a bit of a waste, there was potential for a good character there. She was the only redhead in the story. Scrolling up even further. The words started moving on it's own, leaving me to guess what the words said. I blinked a few times and tried again.
'Thomas t ou he bag oods.' My eyes told me. I knew they were lying. I was at that point of no return.

I looked around the room, trying to refocus them. I balanced my chair on it's two back legs as I leaned slightly backwards. I rubbed my eyes again and pinched the bridge of my nose. Thomas' face was the only clear thing in my mind, I couldn't even see the fucking hand in front of my face that I was waving numbly around. He wasn't even real, my hand was. I felt the balance of the chair shifting and I reached wildly for the table, making the chair even more unbalanced.

"Fuck you," I murmured to the innocent table. With a bang I felt my head hit something and my body probably the floor, but I couldn't tell because the focus was completely lost. The last thing that crossed my mind was Jessica's face, her blue eyes fixed on me.

Chapter two

My head pounded. I rubbed my temples and tried to get up. My body jerked because it didn't know *where* to get up from. I opened my eyes abruptly. I wasn't on the ground. I was far from it, actually. I was standing. The sudden light made me lose sight for a few seconds. That shit was bright, I must've been passed out for a while.

"Are you alright?" I heard a voice say. It sounded familiar, like I've heard it before. Really familiar. I opened my eyes again. No spinning, no dazed feeling of almost passing out. I rubbed the back of my head. I could've sworn I hit it. Pretty hard too. Two blue eyes were fixed on me, together with two dark green ones. They both looked concerned.

"Do you think he can't handle his drink?" the guy began. I looked down. A glass with a see-trough orange drink in it was waiting in my hand. Barely a sip out of it, if there even was one gone at all. Can't handle my drink my ass.

"Come on man, there's barely any gone," I said. I looked at him, then the girl. Jason and Jessica. They were both wearing something completely different from when I saw them this morning. Looked more like party outfits than anything else, a real fancy one though. Didn't look like anything I would ever go to. On top of that, I wouldn't go to anything they were going to. That went both ways, by the way. Jess changed since she got with that dick. Made her a stuck up bitch.

What the hell were they doing here? What was I? I didn't remember ever seeing this room. It was a very big room with a big dark red carpet and even redder curtains.

I closed my eyes for a second and tried to remember what I did to get here. Didn't find anything, but I remembered the fall. *Did* I fall? Maybe I just passed out and fell asleep. I *was* drunk as fuck, maybe I went here after waking up. I had to have been real fucking drunk then, though. Sleepwalking but instead of sleeping I was drunk.

"Where are we?" I said, cutting off Jason who was about to speak again. Jessica put her hand on my shoulder and felt my forehead with her other.
"Are you feeling alright?" she asked again. "Do you want me to get something for you?" I frowned at her and shook her hand off of my shoulder.
"No, I'm fine," I said.

I didn't feel anything from the fall, smelled no vodka either. Maybe I showered before I got here. Would make sense, judging by how fancy I looked. I reached for my head again. I could've sworn there was something. There wasn't, my hand felt nothing. No wound or anything like it. I started to walk towards a chair that was part of a group of chairs, in front of a big fireplace. A few leather chairs, a couple leather couches and some coffee tables with gold decorations. Even though I'd never been there, I could've sworn I knew those chairs. Maybe from my grandma's house. She had big leather chairs. She was dead, though. I rested my hands on the back of the chair. Jessica and Jason walked after me.

"Jess, where are we?" I asked again. I didn't look at her.

14

"Did you call me jazz?" Jason scoffed. What the hell was that guy's problem. I shot him a pissed look but was surprised to see him and Jessica looking back at me, actually confused.

"I think he did," Jessica said.

"Jess, I'm serious, where are we?" Jason and Jessica shot a quick look at each other. A concerned one, this time.

Why the hell were they so god damn concerned? I should be the one being concerned. For all I knew they drugged me. I could have walked in, but I was drunk as a fucking bat right before I fell, so much walking wouldn't have been done. Especially with the clothes we were all wearing. Jason wore a suit, which wasn't unlike him, but I was too. Which was very unlike me. I didn't even own a suit. Maybe I borrowed one from Jason, but why in the god loving fuck would I do that? We didn't even wear the same size, he was taller than I was.

My suit was a dark blue one, close to navy. I wore a light blue shirt underneath the jacket with a navy tie. Jessica wore a dark blue silk dress, which to be fair looked very good on her. I've never seen her wear anything like it. She should've, it looked *really* good. Jason cleared his throat and looked back at me with a slightly condescending look.

"The sitting area," he said. "Where we've been for the past ten or so minutes." I started walking towards the door on the right side of the room. Door is a bit of an overstatement, it was more of a big archway.

"Who's house? Is this yours?" I said. Jason laughed cynically.

"No, knob," he said. I walked through the door. A big hallway with two stairs that connected at the top. It was a bit like a circle.

15

"Who's is it then?" I asked. Why would anyone put so much effort and money in getting me here? Must be a special occasion. I slid my hand along the railing of the stairs. Pure gold probably. Jesus. I heard Jason walk after me, shoes click clacking on the floor.

"What on earth are you doing?" he asked.

"Figuring out where the fuck I am," I said. "Did you kidnap me?"

"Why would I do that? What would I win from that? The pleasure of your company? I'm good without that, thanks."

"I'm not kidding dude, where are we?"

"We're in—," He stopped his sentence as a woman walked into the sitting area with an empty platter, like she was a waitress going back to tables to clean up.

She had a sweet expression, though the main thing I noticed was her red hair. It had a pretty glow over it thanks to the light of the obnoxiously big chandelier that hung in the center of the room. She was pretty but not in the way Jessica was. This one had a bit of a sweet look on her face. Jessica was just hot. No sweet look anywhere on her.

"Ah, perfect timing. Could you get this champ a good old reliable glass of water? He doesn't seem to take his drink well," Jack said.

"Stop with that, ass," I said. "I haven't even taken a sip yet."

"Ah, the man got intoxicated by the smell alone. No more big men's drinks for him." I shot him an angry look.

"You're full of shit," I said and walked back into the sitting room.

"Nancy, did you make any more of these? They were delightful," Jess asked.

16

"I did, would you like another?" Nancy answered. Hold on. I knew a Nancy.
"Nancy?" I asked. Nancy nodded politely and walked over.
"Nancy Jones?" She nodded again.
"Yes sir," she said. Funny coincidence. That's what the maid in my story was called.
"Where is Thomas?" Jack asked. My blood went cold. All down to my fucking toes. There was no way. No god damn way in hell. I looked at Nancy. Exactly as I described her. I looked back at Jason and Jess, then around the room.
"Are you fucking kidding me?" I said. "The count's house?" Jason nodded. I put my hands on my head and looked around in disbelief. Jason grinned.
"See, should've calmed down on the drinks," he said.
"Oh, fuck off, man," I said and sat myself down on the leather chair. Worst thing was that he was technically right. Drinking got me into this shit.
"Excuse me?" He said. His expression changed immediately from gloating to offended. The count's house. I was in my own story.
"Can I be of any help?" Nancy asked.
"Most definitely, he should lay off of the alcohol for a while. Maybe that will help his temper," Jack said, giving me a very obvious side eye.

Fuck. How the hell did I get here? Did I hit my head that hard? Knocking me into another reality? When was I? Was the count already dead?

"Has the count made his announcement already?" I asked.
"Not yet," Joan replied. I was at the start, then. I rubbed my eyes and took a sip of the alcohol in my glass.
"Sir, would you like some water or another beverage instead?" Nancy asked.

"No, it's fine, mister Donovan is overreacting," I said, trying to calm down. I've been in it for just a minute. Jason *already* drove me fucking insane. I didn't know how I got there but I sure as hell didn't want to stay longer than I had to. If I just played along I'd probably get out at the end. I was no expert on getting into your own damn story, ofcourse, but how else *would* I get out? Knocking myself out another time? Jack interrupted me.

"Am I now? Then why are you behaving like a fool?" Stuck in my own story with this dick and my ex.
"I just remembered I had some work to do before tomorrow," I said, then faced Nancy. Had to play the part. "You go on, now." I tried to be as polite as I could while saying it, but still felt like an arrogant ass. Nancy nodded and walked on to the balcony which was through the hallway on the left side of the sitting room. I didn't know much but I spent literal days designing the insides of the house when I was procrastinating the writing. I sighed. The count was probably already dead by now. I came in right 'on time'. God fucking damnit.

A loud, loud scream filled the air. At least I casted her right. Jack and Joan looked up, shocked. As one would be. "What on earth could that be about?" Jack asked. I'd say a death, but it was just a wild guess.
"Nancy, is everything alright?" Joan asked. There was a silence. Jack hurried to the balcony, followed by Joan. Their feet made thumping noises on the carpet. I took a sip of the scotch, might as well. Way better than the cheap vodka I could for some reason barely even remember the taste of.

"Oh my god!" I heard Joan scream.

"Good god, what happened?" Jack said. I really didn't care about the count's death. I knew what happened since I was the detective in a way. I wrote this shit. Badly at that.
"He just collapsed," I heard the count's friend say. Samuel Singretti, the old alcoholic. Like me, but old.
"Do you think it was a heart attack?" Joan said.
"I'm not a bloody doctor, am I?" said Samuel.
"Leonardo," Joan yelled. It was silent for a bit.

Leonardo? I didn't write a character called Leonardo. Did she mean me? I was the only thing different from my original story. I heard Jack walking from the balcony to the room I was in. That man walked very gracefully for someone with a toddler attitude.

"Nardo, we got a problem," he said while looking around the corner. Confused I pointed to me, as to ask if he meant me. He nodded impatiently. I looked at him like he was a little boy who had been naughty.
"Did you cause it?" I asked with a belittling voice. He looked like there was about to be another murder buy didn't say anything back. Nice. He just signaled me to follow him. I raised my hands.
"I really don't care," I said.
"Mate, get the hell out here. This is serious."

A door further down the hall slammed shut and two pair of feet ran across the hall toward the balcony. I knew who it were. Scott and Marilyn, who came from who knows where. Who knows being me and where being the bathroom in the hallway. I even know the what, but I don't kiss and tell for other people. Jack went after them, back to the balcony. I grunted and stood up and walked towards the scene.

Ah god, it was cold outside. I was really tempted to turn back around. There was snow everywhere, except on the covered balcony where the count was laying, dead as a bug. Fun fact, it was so snowy that no one could use the roads, which was convenient because no one could escape even if they tried. With an added bonus of being very visible against the white snow. I would honestly take my losses if I was the killer. There was no way I would go out there.

The wind blew slightly through the doors, making the curtains wave in the wind. Not far from the doorpost stood Joan and Nancy. Nancy was leaning against the doorpost, her face was pale white from the shock. Marilyn, Samuel and Jack stood close to the body and Scott kneeled right next to it.

Marilyn was gorgeous. She was the hoe, the 'femme fatale' as others would call her. She was gorgeous. Her hair was black like... Man, I don't know. It was black, it was shiny, I liked it. She was the opposite of her niece, Joan. Marilyn was the daughter of the count, and the one who probably cared most about the old guy besides maybe Samuel. Her eyes were blue like Joan but darker, with a deeper feel to them. I'm an eye guy, give me a break. Some people are into feet, I'm into eyes. Hers were beautiful. Everyone always wants to be with her or be her, though realistically no one should want either since she's likely got a dictionary worth of STD's. She was a beautiful, beautiful woman. The only one not at the scene was Thomas, the lost relative, once again lost. See what I did there?

Scott had his fingers on the neck of the count. He was checking for pulse, but I could've told him right there the count was dead. Anyone could, he looked as dead as anyone would after dying. The detective, Scott, slowly looked up to the group of people with a sorrowful face. "The count is dead," he said. One thing I *will* say is that it was weird seeing an actual dead body. The only ones I've ever seen were on tv or on the internet, no real ones. I didn't even know the guy, must feel worse for these characters to see. Sucks for them, without his death they wouldn't even be here because there wouldn't be a story to begin with.

Marilyn fell to her knees next to the count and started crying. Tears fell onto the orange-red tiles of the balcony. Scott put his hand on Marilyn's shoulder.
"Was it a heart attack?" Joan asked, again. No tears. Scott shook his head.
"A heart attack does not kill this fast, there are at least minutes before death." He stopped for a second. This was dragging. Man, detective novels are dramatic.
"He's been murdered. The culprit is among us," he said.

There were some scared gasps and some people started looking at one another, probably wondering 'who dun it'. The count, sir Walter Stonier, didn't look at anyone, arrogant ass that he was. His drool slowly started to freeze up and though it didn't look great, I was glad I didn't decide on death by stabbing. That would've been a mess.

As you know, I didn't know what *did* kill him — I hadn't figured that out yet, along with the killer and a fucking plot — but I could see there were no wounds or strangle marks. It was pretty cool seeing what I wrote play out, it didn't all look the same as in my head but at the same time it did. It was kind of like one of those movie adaptations where they got the casting pretty much

21

perfect to what you think they look like in your mind, just a little bit off.

"Joan and Jack, would you please take everyone to the sitting room?" Scott asked.

"Let's get to the sitting area," Joan said to us. She stepped a little further onto the balcony and waved her arms in the way of the room I arrived in.

"What in the bloody hell is he doing?" Samuel asked. Scott had been walking around the house, closing windows and doors.

"Locking the house down so no one can escape," I said.

Everyone turned to look at me. Some looked scared, some annoyed, some were unreadable.

"He thinks one of us did it?" Samuel asked offended. This guy.

"Yes, he does. And I don't blame him, there's no one else that could've done it," Marilyn said.

"There could be an intruder," Jack said.

"All alarms are on. They would have gone off for someone who doesn't know the code," Joan explained.

"One of us can be the intruder. Not everyone is family," Jack said. "And they would want to escape."

"How would we escape, mate. We're snowed in," I said.

"People get crafty when they're threatened," Jack said.

Scott walked into the room and stopped in front of the group. We had been sitting there for a while. I didn't keep track. The only way to know what time it was an old standing clock, but it was right behind me and I didn't feel like turning around every minute.

A lot of the people were talking with each other, I didn't bother to join in. I was almost fully sober, I hadn't been in this state of mind for a long time. It was awful, there was a reason I drank alcohol. This was too thought-y. I could hear my thoughts. Didn't like it very much. The situation itself didn't help. Almost made me panic. Almost. Not the death itself, the being trapped here.

I looked up from my thoughts and at Scott. He was a character that had a natural charisma and leadership vibe to him. He had a very nice face. I did a good job on writing him. His hair was black like Marilyn's. I didn't think anything could escape his gray eyes even if it tried to.

The group fell silent, except for Samuel.
"I'm telling ya, it's suspicious he's not here," he said. Scott cleared his throat and Samuel looked up to him.
"You found the killer?" He asked him.
"I might just be about to," Scott answered. "Mister Singretti, would you please join me in the next room?" Samuel pulled an angry face and turned to Jack who he'd been talking to.
"This guy's got nerves, accusing me." I couldn't help but grin. You had to be there, it was funny.
"For questions, mister Singretti. Nothing more, for now," Scott said and signaled Samuel to follow him.
"Good luck, Sam," Joan said. Samuel stood up and followed but made sure everyone knew he wasn't happy with it. I would bet half my ass that that man was still drunk out of his mind. The other half I would give to be the same thing.

The door with blinds before the window closed behind them. I walked up to it, seeing if I could hear what they were saying. To be very honest, I forgot half the plot of the book. Any bits and pieces I could get, I wanted to take. The people behind me scattered across the room. Nancy

23

walked past me to get more drinks from the kitchen. More alcohol for this bunch of already no longer sober group of traumatized people. Seemed like my kind of people.

"Nar, you coming?" Joan said loudly across the room. I looked back and saw her and Marilyn standing at the door that led to the main staircase and front door, along with some other rooms. I raised my eyebrows at them.
"To where?" I asked.
"To find Thomas," Marilyn said.

Right, I remembered them looking for him. They were alone then, though. Maybe if I went along I would fuck the storyline up. Who knows what would happen. They wouldn't find Thomas, that much I knew. They didn't in the original story either. On the other hand, if I stayed where I was I'd probably do more damage than if I went with the two of them. Fine, I was convinced. Besides, who was I to turn down going with two women who were fucking beautiful? Granted, one was my ex, but there was one that I never even met before.

"I'll be right there," I said. I came closer to the door and heard muffled voices coming from the other side. I couldn't make out what they said. I knew Scott was trying to find motives, and to be fair if anyone could find motives it'd be him. Not to stroke my own ego, but he was me, in a way. Just smarter, and with training to be detective. Samuel's voice became louder but I still couldn't hear what he was saying. Partly because the door muffled the sounds severely, partly because Samuel was so drunk he could barely speak anymore.

Marilyn pulled me away from the door.

"Come," she said. Her eyes glistened. One more look at her and I would. I smirked and walked after her, to find the lost relative or whatever else would come up.

"Do you think Samuel did it?" Joan asked.
"I don't think so, he and my father were very close," Marilyn said.
"But then how would he have died?" Joan said. "Scott said it can't have been a heart attack." She was really holding on to that heart attack.
"And there were no wounds," I added.
"Right!" Joan said. "Besides, I think Samuel was too drunk to kill him." Very likely.
"He wasn't many drinks away from being drunk," Marilyn said. I didn't blame him. I would be too if my best friend died in front of my eyes, even if he was a rich old dick.
"Did either of you actually like him?" I asked.
"Who, Sam?" Joan asked.
"Your uncle."
"What?" Joan asked with the same tone Jessica used when she was upset with me.
"Did either of you actually like him?" Joan very obviously didn't know what to say.
"I did, he was my father," Marilyn said. "Ofcourse I loved him." She looked at Joan and then back at me.
"Did you?" she asked me. Baby, I didn't even know the guy. Not even in terms of writing, all I wrote him as was when he was already dead.
"I didn't know him that well," I said. Joan raised her eyebrows at me as we started walking up the big stairs in the big hallway.

"You were in business with him for years, weren't you?" she said. Fucking hell, I had a backstory.
"Right, but I never saw him outside business."

Not only did I now have to not fuck the story up, I had to be someone I didn't even know. Was Leonardo even real? Outside this shit? Why couldn't I have come in as Scott like normal 'sucked into story' stories do. I could've figured this shit out myself. Would give me some extra height too.

"Where could Thomas be?" Marilyn asked.
"Lets check the room where Nancy lived before they married, first," Joan said.

The mansion was huge, there were so many rooms it could pass for a tiny hotel. I doubt all of them were in use, there weren't that many people living at the mansion. Just family, and Joan didn't even live there anymore ever since she married Jack. It was weird that I remembered all of our shit together from the real world and she didn't. This Joan was more like Jess before we met. Less of a bitch, more like a normal person.

The walls of the upstairs layer of the house were decorated with weird art, some from Joan's collection, some from Walter's. Joan was a collector of art and antiques, when I started writing the story I thought that'd fit her since she loved history. I'm glad this job wasn't the one she actually had, I didn't want any of these paintings in my own house. I saw one with a horse without head, with a rider on top dressed in roses. One with a large hedge maze, like the ones they have at old castles, with in front of the opening a child with a lollipop made of dogs. It's your stock photo variant of mystery novel paintings.

"Jesus," I murmured. Marilyn, who walked next to me, looked at me with an asking look. I just pointed to the painting. She grinned and nodded.

"Artistic," she said. I grinned back.

Joan led the way, almost speed walking towards Nancy's room. She put her hand on the door handle and waited for Marilyn and I. She pushed the handle down and the door creaked open, revealing a dark room. Unless he was hiding in the dark, he wasn't in this room. I knew he wasn't, I remembered — yes, remembered, believe it or not — him being in a shed just a couple of feet from the mansion. I think he was trying to fix a knife for Nancy. One to cut cake with rather than people though. Could be used for both if you got a little creative but it wasn't like that.

"Thomas?" Joan called out to the obviously empty room.
"I don't think he's here, honey," Marilyn said. She put her hand on Joan's shoulder and guided her away. It didn't look like that in my head when I wrote it. She was almost eager to leave the room. What the fuck could be in there that I didn't know about? A quick look couldn't hurt.
"I'll be right out," I said, and went into Nancy's room. Marilyn's eagerness made me suspicious. Always follow your gut.

"Don't you think we should keep looking?" She asked, her hand now on *my* shoulder, gently pulling me away. "I doubt he'll appear in there."
"I won't be in there for long, you can check the next room if you want, might save time," I insisted.
"Do you want me to come with you?" Marilyn asked, but Joan shook her head.

"No, It's better to split up. We'll check a room each. See you in five, Nardo," she said after which she pulled Marilyn with her. Marilyn shot one last look at me and then disappeared behind a corner of the hallway, onto the next room.

Chapter three

With a swift movement I pushed the big wooden door open further and flicked the light on. Slowly, I walked into Nancy's room. She didn't do it, I was almost fully sure. A wave of sweet perfume hit me when I stepped into the room a bit farther. Don't ask me what kind, I don't know shit about women's perfume. It did smell nice, though, intense as it was. She liked her perfume, that was for sure. I switched the light switch on the wall on and the crystal lamp on the ceiling turned on. Even though this room was one of the smaller ones because it was for a staff member, it was still a lot bigger than my living room.

There were books everywhere. On the dresser, the small desk, some on the floor. None on the neatly made bed, though it seemed like there hadn't been anyone sleeping it for a long while. That checked out, she probably lived with Thomas now. No need to sleep in this bed when she could sleep in one that had a guy in it. Her husband, at that. Easy choice.

Don't kill me for the spoiler but she died later in the story. That's one of the only things I remembered. Good to remember, too. I wanted to stay as far away from it as possible. I didn't know who or what killed her, so better be safe than sorry. I didn't feel like dying in the crossfire of this shit show, whether it was real or not. It was weird seeing her things. I thought it'd be fine to kill her since she was only the maid. The screaming one, I might add. Adds a bit of extra annoying. She wasn't. She seemed pretty nice. Smart, too, judging by the books. Something a lot of the people here weren't. Including me, don't think I felt better than them.

The dresser had a lot of stuff on it. Besides the books there were some solid white colored bottles and a lot of loose paper with things written on them. I grabbed one of the sheets of paper. The writings were almost math like, though I couldn't read what it said. I wasn't a wiz in maths. She either had a really bad handwriting, or I just didn't know the language.
"What the fuck," I whispered. I put the paper back where it came from and picked up one of the bottles. It felt as cold as the bottle of vodka had felt. I heard the noise of something moving inside as I gently shook it. It sounded like small marbles, glass-like, maybe plastic. I unscrewed the lid and put it on the dresser, on top of a stack of books. She had some pretty big names gathered in her room, an impressive collection for a maid. She seemed to be into science.

I looked inside the bottle and shook it gently. Layers and layers of little dark brown-yellow pills. I didn't recognize them. I wasn't from this time, though, so might be just a time thing. Were either Nancy or Thomas sick? I must admit I didn't spend a lot of time on it, but I was pretty sure everyone was healthy. Maybe it were some type of cosmetic pills, I've read a lot of weird stories from the past. They even used the juice of a poisonous plant as eyedrops to make their pupils bigger. Was supposed to be a sign of attraction because your pupils get bigger when you look at something you love.
I put my finger in the bottle and churned around a bit. It didn't do anything special.

"Have you found him?" I heard a voice saying softly after which the light went out. Jesus christ, I almost dropped the bottle. I turned around and saw Marilyn standing right by the doorpost, blocking the light from the hallway a little bit. I could make out a smile on her face, probably there because of my reaction. I gathered my thoughts and frowned. I missed the question.

"What?" I asked.
"Thomas, have you found him hidden under the bed?" She replied. She slowly walked towards me, not taking her eyes away from mine. I knew this thing that she did. I grinned.
"Sadly no, I haven't yet," I said. "But we can check the bed again if you want." Marilyn's eyes swayed downwards, but instead of their expected path back up to my eyes they made a turn and went to the bottle in my hand.
"What's that?" She asked.
"Pills," I said. Her face didn't change.
"Do you know what they are?" She raised her eyebrows and held out her hand. I handed her the bottle. Her face was unreadable when she looked inside.
"I'm not sure, it could be anything. Maybe they're for her cat."
"Why would she keep those here?"
"She keeps everything here." She handed me the bottle and her hand lingered for a second.

My eyes were drawn to hers like magnets. The light from the hallway that creeped through the small gap between the door and the doorpost lit up half of her face. She genuinely *was* beautiful. There were worse people to be in a dark room with. I picked up the lid of the bottle and screwed it back on without looking away from Marilyn. I did way too good a job at writing her. At least one thing I didn't fuck up in this story.

She took the bottle and put it back on the dresser. I put my hand behind her waist, slowly pulling her in. Should I? I could barely even think. I barely even wanted to. Thinking would fuck shit up. She put her hands over my shoulders and grinned. With my free hand I pushed a strand of hair behind her ear and grabbed her face, pulling it toward mine. I felt her breath on my face. I knew she wasn't real, but she didn't make it feel anything like it. Her lips locked with mine. Good lord. For a character in a book she was a real good kisser. Her arms on my shoulders pulled us even closer together. I felt her body against mine. My ability to think was completely gone, all my thinking went downwards. My hand traced her back, slowly reaching her ass.

"Marilyn?" Joan said, bursting into the room, flicking on the lights. Marilyn and I broke apart, looking like teenagers who were just caught by a parent. Joan's eyes widened and she stopped moving.
"Oh," she said. I coughed and focused on one of the papers on the dresser. Marilyn and Joan exchanged looks, which I only saw from the corner of my eye. In this story me and Jessica were never together but the feeling of your ex walking in while you're with another girl is an awful fucking feeling, whether the ex realized she was your ex or not. I felt them looking at me and I looked up from the paper.
"The man's not here," I said, to break the silence.
"No, I think he is," Joan said looking at me, glancing down. Right, the annoying chick. She played the part just perfect. I looked at Marilyn, who tried to hide a smile. So much for support, nice.

"Right, did *you* find him then?" I asked Joan. Trick question, I knew she hadn't. She shook her head. Would be something if she did find him. Surprise, I'd have fucked up the story.

"I didn't. Do you think he is even upstairs?" she asked.

"There aren't any more rooms he really uses."

"I wonder if he's even in the house," Marilyn said. "I saw him half an hour ago but I'm not ruling out the possibility of him escaping if he murdered my father." I shrugged and walked towards the door.

"If," I said. I heard Marilyn follow.

I walked trough the archway leading to the sitting room, Marilyn walking next to me and Joan as before walking in front of us.

"I thought I told everyone to stay in here," Joan said. The sitting room was empty.

"You can't expect a guy like Jack to listen, the guy is a menace," I said.

"We left too," Joan said.

"Yes, to find someone to bring back," Marilyn said. Exactly.

"Fine. Alright. Well, I think Nancy is in there with Scott," Joan said. "But I don't know where the other three are."

She could be in there, she could be dead already. I had no idea. Though to be fair, in my original story the point of view was the detective, so most of the time of the first bit of the book was talking to people in that tiny office like he was with Samuel before. This was the only time Samuel was a suspect. He really didn't have a motive. He was just there. Bad writing at my part, I guess. Lazy.

"Do you figure she did it?" Marilyn asked.

"Nancy?" I asked, genuinely surprised. Unless she helped her husband get away with it I doubted she knew

33

anything. That and the fact she died later. Fun little surprise. Marilyn nodded.

"Have you met her?" Joan replied. "She's an angel."

"You know demons were angels that fell down, right," Marilyn said.

"Why would Nancy do such a thing?" Joan asked.

Marilyn draped herself on the couch and picked up a drink from Nancy's tray that was left on the table. I couldn't look away.

"Why would *any* of us?" She said. Joan rolled her eyes.

"I'm going to go find Jack," she said and walked off. Marilyn sighed dramatically.

"I'm done finding people. Now I want them to find me," she said. She looked seductively at me. I laughed and sat down on the couch next to her. It was between this or walking with my ex to find the guy she was fucking. Wasn't a very hard choice.

"Right, my turn to find you," I said with a grin bigger than planned.

"I think you've already found me," she said and bit her lip. Fuck this story, man. Why couldn't there be a Marilyn in my real life?

"If you keep biting your lip, I'm gonna do it for you."

Don't worry, we didn't do anything. She just rested her head on my shoulder and went silent for a minute. I didn't bother to do anything. Scott was in the office right next to us.

"It's odd to think he's still laying outside in the cold," Marilyn said after a while.

Right. I didn't feel the situation as much as she probably did. My dad didn't just die. I nodded. It was a weird thought, a dead guy just outside of the window. Fiction or not, dead is dead. Didn't happen everyday that there's a

34

body just a couple of feet away from you. The balcony went around the entire backside, so if we looked out of the huge window and a little bit downwards at the floor we would no doubt see him.

"I don't think Scott would like it if we pulled him inside, though," I said. She raised her eyebrows and laughed. "He'd go mad," she said. "Even touching him would mean we 'distorted the crime scene'."
Marilyn rested her head on my shoulder again.
"He is a very clever man. I trust him to solve the murder."
"Hmm," I hummed in agreement. Scott was a good piece of writing too. Besides, his brain was even better than his looks. That's saying something.
"If he couldn't I don't know who could," I said.

Joan walked into the room, followed by Jack and mister Singretti. She had a habit of walking in front of people, apparently. Dominant daddy that she was.
"Is that bastard done with the girl yet?" Samuel asked.
Marilyn rolled her eyes.
"He's not a bastard," she said.
"Not yet," I said, though replying to Samuel, not Marilyn.
Samuel sat down in the chair next to me.
"I don't like him one bit," Samuel replied.
"Geez, Sam. I know," Marilyn said.

He was a pretty old man, used to be an archeologist. A good one, by the way. The man has been all over the world, discovering cool things, making him famous pretty much instantly. He's been retired for a long ass time now which made him bored and an alcoholic. That's what I wanted to be as a kid, an archeologist. Well, I was halfway there already. To be Sam, at least. I had the alcoholic part down.

35

Jack put his arm around Joan and gave her a kiss on the cheek. Jackass. I knew they weren't real, but the sight of Jack kissing Joan was *revolting*.

"Where have the both of ya been anyway?" Samuel said to Marilyn and I. Joan shot Marilyn a knowing look.
"Looking for Thomas," I replied quickly.
"Found 'm yet?" Samuel said.
"Obviously not," Marilyn said, gesturing to the Thomas-less room. Samuel looked a bit offended at first but then started laughing with us.
"Where have you been, then?" Marilyn asked.
"We did a bit of poker until Joanie came in," Samuel replied. "I was winning."
"Cheating, the good man was cheating," Jack corrected him. Oh, the irony. Samuel laughed.
"Can't handle his loss."
"I bloody well can, but it's a bit hard to win against a cheater now, isn't it?"
"It's only cheating if you get caught."
"I *did* catch you, remember? That's why I'm calling you out on it."
"We are in the middle of an investigation, we have bigger issues than poker," Joan interrupted.
"We can have a little bit of-," Samuel said, waving his hand around in the air, as if reaching for the word. "-Fun, can't we, Joanie?"

The door of the side room swung open and Nancy came out, pale as a sheep. Scott appeared behind her, calm as ever. He really *was* handsome. Nancy walked up to the sitting area, grabbed the tray she had left when she was called in and sort of faced us. She didn't really look any of us directly in the eye.
"Can I get anyone anything?" She asked.

"We're fine," Joan said. "Why don't you join us? It beats waiting around in the kitchen alone. Besides, you deserve it. You've been preparing for days."

"No, that's okay. I'll start taking out something to eat while we wait," she said.

"Actually, you can bring me another drink," Jack said.

Nancy nodded and walked towards the kitchen.

"Mister Berratare, please join me," Scott said. Must be me, I didn't write anyone with that last name. I stood up and sighed.

"Time to fess up to your sins," Jack said and put his thumb up.

"Oh, fuck off," I said. Samuel winked at me. An old man wink to wish you luck, rather than inviting you to fuck. So I hoped, at least.

I walked into the small room with blinds in front of the window of the door. You know, like in detective movies. Scott closed the door behind me, making the blinds clap against the window. Even though I knew Scott was in some way me, I still felt like I was about to get a lecture from a principal. He gestured to the chair in front of the desk.

"Take a seat," he said. His voice even sounded a bit like mine, though deeper and with more authority. He waited until I sat down and then sat down on the chair behind the desk. He was a tall man, at least six feet two. I was a little nervous. Definitely felt some nerves tingling inside me. I could accidentally make him think I did it instead of him finding the real killer if I wasn't careful with my answers.

I sat down and kept my eyes on Scott. Did that seem suspicious? I hadn't even done anything but forgot how to

37

act nonetheless. Ironic. The leather chair was still warm from Nancy and Samuel who sat in it before me. I looked at him patiently while he organized his notes and flipped a notepad to a blank page.

"Let's start, shall we?" he started, looking at me with his intense, gray eyes. "Where were you at the time of discovery?" His pen clicked open, his face stood friendly but determined.
"Do I really have to do this?" I asked. He smiled a quick smile.
"It would be odd not to question you, wouldn't it? I'm questioning everyone, after all."
"In the sitting area," I sighed. "With Jack and Joan." He nodded and wrote some words down on a separate piece of paper. Did I do good, dad?
"What is your occupancy?" He asked. I just stared at him, blank faced. I didn't fucking know, I wasn't 'mister Berratare'.
"Leonardo," Scott said. I snapped out of it.
"I'm in trades," I said. Scott scribbled something down.
"Where is your place of residence and of business?"
"I live in London, my place of business is there as well," I said.

This backstory annoyed me. I didn't even know if it was true. Imagine if it wasn't, I'd instantly become the most suspicious person. Lying in an investigation.

"Have you been around the kitchen area in the hour before?" He asked.
"I haven't," I said. For as far as I knew.
"Have you had any hand in obtaining or preparing either the whiskey or the cigars the count used?"

"No," I said. "Do you think someone put something in there?"

He didn't reply. Which, in itself, was a reply. Good to know, he thought the count was killed by poisoning. Seemed like an either great or horrible way to die, depending on the poison. Which, of course, I had no idea of what it was. Same with the killer. Wish I had, though, that would've made being here a lot easier. I'd know who not to piss off.

"What is your relation to the count?"
"We're business associates."
"So I've heard. However I would like to hear about your personal relationship with mister Stonier." His face didn't give anything away, half of the time examining me, the other half writing down things on multiple notes.
"It was mostly business related, though I've been to a lot of the parties the count had," I said.
"You were not part of mister Stonier's will, correct?" He asked. I wish, the guy was loaded.
"Indeed," I said.
"What haunts you?" He asked. Fuck, I forgot about these questions. What the hell was I supposed to say? Bloody Mary? Scott looked at me and gave me a smile.
"It could be anything," he said. "For some it may be the death of someone, for others it may be a choice they made."
"You want me to answer what haunts me?"
"I do." I nodded slowly. Ah well. Why the fuck not.
"Not reaching the full potential I know I have," I said. Mostly true, fit the character too. Probably. I didn't know the character that well yet. Had to do some developing.
"What is your greatest strength?"
"My perfectionism," I said.

39

"And weakness?"

"The same thing."

"Alright," Scott said as he wrote down on the notepad.

"I imagine that can be hard at times," he said, looking up for a second. "Surely can be useful, but particularly draining as well." Therapy rather than principal's lecture, even better. I didn't say anything.

"And your greatest fear?"

"My greatest fear?" I repeated. Scott just nodded.

"Right," I started and thought for a second. "No one remembering me after my death." Scott scribbled something again. It's a smart way to get to the murderer, analyzing their psychology, I had to give him that. Or me, actually, since I wrote him.

"Nancy told me you were... agitated, right before the discovery of the body," he said. Huh. Did she now. Just threw me under the bus. "Can you tell me what happened?"

"I remembered I had an important deal I had to close before the morning, one I could no longer finish in time," I said. "Is there anything else?"

"I was about to ask you the same question," he said. "Did you come across anything you think to be of importance?" I did, matter of fact. I had a bus too.

"There were some pills in Nancy's room, I saw them when I went to find Thomas," I said. "Jones. Thomas Jones." Scott's face didn't give anything away but I felt the tension rise. Might've been something else, Scott was too good-looking for my own good.

"How did you come across these pills?" He asked.

"I was curious to see what was inside the bottles, considering there has been a murder. Anything can be a clue."

40

"Certainly, but usually it's up to the investigator to investigate," he said with a little smile. "Now could you describe the pills for me?"

"Brownish, small round pills."

"Did they give off any particular smell?"

"Not that I'm aware of, no," I said. "But I didn't smell them." Scott nodded slowly.

"That's good of you. After the interviews, could you take me to see them? I would like to have a closer look at them."

"Yeah, sure," I said. "Just say the word and I'll take you up there." Take that however you like.

"Much appreciated. I might ask you to come in again later, so please do stay seated in the sitting area." He stood up and opened the door.

The group of people in the sitting area were facing a man who I hadn't seen before. Thomas, the lost — now found — relative. A tall guy with dark blond hair and a pretty strong build. These men were tall, I wish I wrote them a bit shorter so I could have a sense of, I don't know, safety.

"Ah, the person I was hoping to talk to next," Scott said, standing right behind me. I walked back to the leather couch and sat down. Thomas was even taller than Scott, and had a face just as pretty.

"Mister Chase, I assume? A pleasure," Thomas said and walked towards Scott to shake his hand. "I've heard nothing but good about you."

"Likewise, mister Jones. Great to have you."

Samuel stood up from the leather chair he was sitting in and sat down next to me on the couch. Thomas and Scott walked into the small room that had changed into the detective's office and closed the door.

41

"So, how did it go?" Samuel asked.

"It went alright, his technique is good," I said.

"Good for you," Samuel said and took another big sip of his whiskey. "I don't like him one bit." Marilyn rolled her eyes.

"So you've said."

"I have and I will again. He's a weird type, that one. Kept asking me stupid questions. He saw where I was when it happened, didn't he?" Samuel said. "Didn't have to bloody ask. It's like asking someone what they're drinking after you yourself poured it."

"At least he didn't die alone," I said. A grateful smile came over Samuel's face and he put his hand on my shoulder. He nodded.

"And thank god for that," he said. "No one deserves that."

It was his biggest fear, dying alone.

"Some people do," Jack said.

"No they don't, it's worse than death," Samuel replied.

"I severely doubt that, my good man," Jack hummed.

"Who do all of you think did it?" Marilyn asked.

"That's the question you're asking around people who are all suspects?" Samuel asked. "Now you're being stupid."

"It's my father, I am allowed to wonder who murdered him in cold blood."

"I think it's Thomas," Jack remarked. He received a soft slap from Joan.

"Jack!" She said. He shrugged.

"His reasons are obvious," he said. "Nancy mentioned they were about to be evicted from their property."

"Really?" I asked.

They were. Bakery and house combined, the count didn't want to help even though Thomas was his nephew. There's something to be said for being self sustaining but this was more a dick-move than anything else. Jack nodded.

"Briefly, but Thomas wouldn't kill someone over something like that," Joan said. "I doubt he would ever even kill anyone at all. Especially family."

"He might, he only discovered we were his family two years ago," Marilyn said.

"Family is family," Joan said. "Time means less than that."

"Who do you think did it, then?" Jack asked. Joan's eyes briefly went to me but they flicked away when she realized I saw her looking. She stayed silent.

"Me?" I asked, a bit more offended than necessary.

"Well no, not really, of course. I mean, you're the only one who's not family, you know. I don't *really* think you would murder anyone." I saw Jack smile. Was he enjoying her accusing me?

"Jesus, Joan," I said.

"Who do you think did it, Nardo?" Marilyn asked.

"Joan," I replied. Two can play that game. Did I really think she did it? No. I still thought Thomas or Jack did it. It made the most sense. Either one. Maybe even together.

"You were right here with us when he died mate," Jack said. Even in my book this jackass called me mate. "How could she have killed him?" Marilyn laughed.

"As bright as ever," she said. "By your logic Leonardo couldn't have done it either, he was with you."

Jack shot her an angry look. I don't think Jack even slightly liked Marilyn. Jack rose up and held out his hand to Joan, nudging toward the entrance.

"I wish you all a good time waiting until Marilyn's date comes to fetch you, but there's no need to stay here together. Come, Joan," he said.

"You can't leave!" Marilyn said.

"We won't leave the property if that's what you're afraid of."

"He said to stay put here," Marilyn said, "So that's what we'll do, dear Jack. I don't care if you want to get out of here, there is a murder investigation going on. You're not going to solve it by shagging my niece."

"But neither are we while waiting around."

"This way we at least won't make it worse."

"You just might," Jack said and walked out of the room, Joan shortly after following him.

"He's such an arse," Marilyn said to me.

"I heard that," Jack said from the hallway.

"You were supposed to," Marilyn replied with a fake smile.

"I don't like seeing them together," I said. Even though it had been a few years since Jessica left me for that guy, I've never had to see it up close.

"Why not?" Sam asked. He had a confused look on his face. Right, this Joan was different. Joan has never had another man besides Jack.

"She reminds me of my ex," I said. Wasn't lying. "It's very weird to see." I felt Marilyn's hand glide on my thigh. I inhaled sharply and looked at the ceiling for a second. Focus, brother. Keep it down for gods sake.

"Exes are exes for a reason," she said. Samuel's face looked even more confused.

"Say, Marilyn, weren't you with Scott?" he said, then laughed. "Forget what I said, Nardo is an upgrade." Marilyn smiled and stroked my leg.

"Like you said earlier, Singretti. We can have a little fun, can't we?" He threw a pillow.

"Yes, but don't have fun in front of me, for the love of god." He jokingly put his hand in front of his eyes and pulled a disgusted face. I grinned and heard Marilyn laugh.

"See, you're fun. Jack's gone for less than five minutes and the energy has shifted," Marilyn said.

"What's with you and Jack anyway?" I asked her. "I don't like him either but you seem to actually *hate* the man."

"I don't hate him, I just strongly dislike him. Joan can do better than him."

"Now that I agree with."

"I like him," Samuel said. Marilyn rolled her eyes again.

"Of course you do. You dislike Scott and like Jack."

"Damn right I hate that Scott-figure. Why didn't we call the police instead of this guy?"

"Even if we did, they wouldn't be here in time. At least until tomorrow, the roads are blocked thanks to the snow, remember?" Marilyn said. "We are very lucky that Scott is here." I nodded.

"I heard a lot of great stories about his previous cases," I added.

The door of the side room swung open and Thomas strutted out.

"Marilyn, Scott wants you to come in," he said.

"Speak of the devil," Samuel said. Thomas frowned when he saw the room empty besides the three of us.

"Didn't Scott say to stay here?" He said.

"That's what I said," Marilyn said and stood up. She walked towards Thomas and the door.

It's never been this hard to not look at someone walking away. She closed the door behind her, making the blinds tap the window. Thomas caught me staring.

"Don't look into her eyes, she might steal your soul," he said and sat down on a leather chair. Samuel laughed.

"He's too busy with her behind to look her in the eyes," he said.

"Well," I said laughing. "She has a very nice one."

"I thought so too until I found out she was my cousin," Thomas said.

"Jesus," I said. "Have you ever-?"

45

"Once, yeah. Has Nancy popped in yet?" He asked, eyeing the kitchen.

"No she hasn't yet, I don't think. Actually, she was going to get Jack another drink. She hasn't brought it yet," I said. My mind rewinded. Did he say he fucked his cousin?

"I'll be damned, you're right," Samuel said. Thomas nodded slowly and raised his eyebrows, after which he placed his hands behind his head and leaned back.

"I haven't spoken to her in a while," he said. "I better check up on her soon."

He eyed me and nodded towards the hallway. What, he wanted to fuck me too? I wasn't family, was I?

"You wanna go and find Joan and Jack first? I wager Scott wants to speak to them sooner rather than later."

"Ah sure thing, he's spoken to me already anyway. Does Joan still have a room in this house?" I asked.

"What, you think they're shagging?" Thomas said. "That'd be inconsiderate regarding the circumstances, don't you think?" Almost as inconsiderate as fucking your cousin, yeah. Weird family, weird weird family.

Chapter four

The hallway was quieter than it was the last time I walked there. The wind had calmed down and no longer howled for attention. The music that played in the sitting room was barely even noticeable here, even though it was just a few feet away. We walked up the big stairs again. The width of the stairs was longer than Thomas was tall, rich people have such unnecessary shit in their houses.

The slight heel on my shoes hitting the floor was the only sound that stood out against the silence. They were like tap-dance shoes, just for suits. Whoever Leonardo was, style was not one of his greater qualities. Thomas walked next to me and had something of a jog going, almost running up the stairs. Eager guy. Didn't hear a sound from him, though.

The balcony that connected the stairs had some kind of drapes hanging in front of it, like long curtains, that reached from the ceiling to the ceiling of the hallway. There were those rope-like things to open it on both sides and one in the middle, all gold.
We walked past the big vases with roses in them that stood at the top of both staircases. I'm personally not big on flowers but I gotta admit, these roses smelled amazing. The paintings on the walls on this side of the building were equally as ugly as the ones on the side where Nancy used to sleep together with the other staff that coincidentally weren't here today. The count had given them a day off because this was a family only type of

gathering, to reveal something. Of course, no one knew what exactly since the count tragically passed away before revealing the news. Even I didn't know, I didn't write that part because the count died. I wanted to let it unfold naturally without scripting and planning too much. May not have been the brightest idea, considering I was *in* the book now, would've been great to have a bit of a heads-up.

"You think we should knock?" Thomas asked, piercing the silence we had going on.
"Are you kidding? Yeah, fucking knock. I don't wanna see him butt naked," I said. I didn't wanna see Jack at all, to be fair. "I have to see that dickhead the whole evening, I don't feel much for seeing that *actual* dick head."
"Right, I thought so," Thomas laughed and knocked on the door with his knuckles. "That was a good one." The rustling inside stopped.
"Who's there?" I heard Joan say.
"It's us," Thomas said.
"Scram," Jack said and the rustling continued, though this time it sounded more like clothes than sheets. Thomas waited ten seconds and then walked into the room.
"Mate, what the hell do you think you're doing?" Jack said, standing in the middle of the room. He had one arm in his shirt but that was pretty much it. Cheeks out and all.
"Ah god," I said and looked away out of instinct.
"Don't try to act like that mate," Jack said. "I look damn good." I didn't see his face —or any of him for that matter — but his voice sounded mad. Mad annoying, too. Piece of shit.
"Get your fucking clothes on," I said.
"Bet I look better than you, is why you're ashamed, aren't you?"
"Are you fucking serious?" I said, and looked him right in the eye. Joan was right behind him, trying to cover herself

48

with the sheets. I walked into the room, past Thomas, and threw Joan her dress. She mouthed thanks.

"Show me then," Jack said, still only one arm in the shirt. I looked at him like he was crazy. He was dead serious.

I heard Thomas laugh softly and looked back at him. He just raised his hands in the air as a sign I was in it alone and continued laughing. Jack looked at me smugly, not once breaking eye contact. Joan hadn't said a word since we came in, just looking embarrassed, avoiding eye contact with both me and Thomas. Who, by the way, still just stood by the door, not doing anything.

"What are you saying, man?" I said.
"I challenge you, since you think you look better than me. Thomas and Joan will decide."
"I must say, Jack does look good for a lad," Thomas said, only putting oil on the fire.
"What, you want to see me naked too?" I said, turning to him, continuing in my talk-to-cat voice. "You want to see my little Nardo, huh?" Jack and Thomas started laughing, I couldn't help but join in. The genre was detective story, as far as I knew, not whatever the fuck this was. I knew for *sure* I didn't write this shit. This was stupid.
"Your little Nardo," Thomas laughed.
"The both of you are mad, now go on and get dressed, you weird cunt," I said to Jack.
"And?" He said. I dramatically looked around the room and threw my arms in the air.
"Fine. You win. You have the prettiest cock." The guy grinned and put his other arm in his shirt.
"Biggest balls too," he said.
"Like baseballs," Thomas said. "Incredible." His grin was just as big as Jack's. Bunch of wankers. Joan stood up and walked past Thomas, through the door.

49

"I thought he was into women only, but c'est la vie," she said, looking around the edge of the door, and then disappeared downstairs.

"It's alright mate, I'll see you naked some other time," Jack said, ignoring — or maybe adding to — Joan's comment.

"Now no one will know what your little Nardo looks like," Thomas said. "Though if you keep doing what you're doing, I think Marilyn may find out. I'll just ask her." Jack stopped mid pants and raised one of his eyebrows.

"Marilyn? You got a thing going with Marilyn?"

"I know she's with Scott and I respect the man so I don't think I'll do anything. Now keep going with your pants," I started.

"Nah, you can't," Jack said and continued pulling his pants up. "Don't fuck with Marilyn. I feel sorry for Scott, Marilyn is one crazy woman. Don't fuck with that."

"She doesn't seem that bad," I said. It wasn't just Marilyn who didn't like jack, then. Jack didn't like her guts either. Thomas interrupted.

"She's not crazy, she's passionate."

"Same thing, mate, same bloody thing. I'm glad Joan didn't come from Stonier's sack, she's the opposite of Mari," Jack said. "She's the princess, Mari is the evil queen. The type that steals your happiness."

"Evil queens are the princesses that were never saved," Thomas said.

"And solitude drives the most sane people insane, so it doesn't matter how she started. All that matters is how she is now," jack said.

"Huh, remarkably poetic. I'll give you that. Now get your things on and get downstairs before Scott kicks your pretty ass."

"Yeah yeah. I'm already on my way," he replied and put on his suit jacket. "I think he can wait one minute." He tied his shoes and walked toward the door. He turned around briefly, winked, and left.

"See you in a bit," he said from the hallway.

"Good luck," Thomas said.

"Weird motherfucker," I said.

"Ah, a little bit. It would be boring without him, though."

"Ha, you can say that again."

"You up for a game of cards?" Thomas said, then gestured me to get out the room so he could close the door. "Beats waiting around."

"Yeah, sure. You wanna get a cocktail downstairs?" I asked.

"I've had enough cock for at least a minute," Thomas said. Funny, actually. The npc's were unlocking humor. "I'm more of a whiskey lad anyway. I think the dead man has some good liquid in his office. He's not coming back to use it, would be a waste to leave it standing around." He started walking in the direction of Walter's office. I frowned and walked after him.

"Isn't that a little soon?" I said. The count was still laying dead, outside in the cold. His whiskey would be gone before the blood even puddled down in his body.

"Never too soon for whiskey, my friend."

"If you say so," I said. It wasn't my uncle. I could use some whiskey to be honest, it's been at least half an hour since my last drink. Some sort of cocktail Nancy had made. Really good for this era of humanity but it didn't beat the shit from the real world.

The door of Walter's office was the biggest one in the hallway, along with the one to his chambers. Big door, big ego, seemed about right. Remember what I said about big coats? Same thing. Thomas swung the door open with the same ease he swung the door downstairs, the one Scott used for his 'office', though this one was considerably

51

heavier. He could kill me in a second and I wouldn't realize it until I saw the pearly gates. I wasn't weak by any means, but Jesus fuck, I needed to write weaker characters.

The room itself smelled like cigars, which wasn't a surprise, considering the man was a chain-smoker. Good quality cigars, ofcourse, but way too many. It was a surprise he hadn't died of that before I killed him off. I tried smoking once a long time ago but it wasn't my thing. Glad it wasn't, unhealthy and expensive shit. Alcohol is expensive enough, let alone if I smoked cigs too. I'd be broke.

The desk stood in the centre of the room, with the chair of it directly behind it with the back facing the window. Expensive wood, probably. Looked like cherry wood, that beautiful red wood. I got a side table of it in my own house, which was way smaller yet still way too fucking expensive for a table.

There were files spread over the desk like Walter just got up and left it like that. He probably did. On the left side of the room there was a huge closet-like thing with glass in the doors so you could see the massive amount of bottles of whiskey and cigars inside. There were some huge bottles and some very tiny ones, but almost all were barely drunken out of. There was a couch stood next to it. A green with red one.

"See, some very good bottles in there." Thomas walked over to it and after scanning the shelves he took out a big, decorated bottle with more than half of the whiskey already gone. He took two glasses from the lower shelf and gestured to the desk.

52

"Let's try this one. Can you clear some of those?" I walked over to the desk and did exactly that.

"Is it a good one?" I asked while putting some of the files on the chair behind the desk.

"The best, man. Way too expensive for a whiskey, but amazing. If it weren't for unc Walt I would've never tried it." He put the glasses on the desk and poured the whiskey in.

"Have you had this one before, Nardo?"

"Don't think I have, I think I'd recognize that bottle. Besides, I usually buy cheaper shit," I said and sat down on the edge of the desk. He handed me the glass and clinked his against mine.

"Well, to our health. That we may live long and not die the way Walt died," he said. I scoffed. This guy didn't give a shit.

"To our health," I said.

It was a strong whiskey, better than any I tasted before. Beats the cheap vodka by a hundred.

"Jesus Christ, it's amazing," I said while I put the glass back with a slam to cover up the face I was about to make.

"Told you," Thomas grinned.

"Where the hell did he get whiskey this good?"

"I think Joan did, actually. She finds them on her 'treasure-hunts', as she calls them."

"Ah right, she's into antiques." I wish Jessica had been, maybe she'd find great whiskey too. The buzz of the whiskey slowly got to my head.

"It's fast, man," I said. He held out the bottle.

"Another one?" He said. I smirked and gestured to my glass, which he poured.

"To Joan," I said.

"To Joan, and her treasure-hunts." The second buzz came even sooner than the first one did.

"Powerful one," Thomas said. We put our glasses down on the desk again.

"Man, tell me about it. The last time I had a buzz this quick was years ago."

"You should buy better alcohol, then," Thomas joked. I picked up one of the papers, trying to see if I could still read it with the early buzz. I couldn't.

"Is it anything interesting?" Thomas asked, clearly feeling the buzz too.

He sat down on the desk and looked over to the papers. I tried reading it by squinting my eyes. Maybe if I squinted hard enough I'd wake up in the story of that paper, happened once, might happen again. 'Appointed shares STR', I could make out.

"Some business-shit," I said.

"What kind?" He asked.

"Shares in a company," I said. Thomas handed me another glass of whiskey. I downed it in a second and read ahead. I really shouldn't be gulping them down as quick as I did.

"As far as I can see it's name is 'Donovan steel'," I said. Donovan. Wasn't Jack—

"Donovan steel? Are you sure?" Thomas said.

"Yeah, look," I said, putting the paper in front of his eyes.

"Isn't that Jack's dad's company?" Thomas nodded and looked focused — or made a good attempt to.

"It is, and as far as I can see it's a big amount of shares too," he said. "Depending on how many Jack has, he might even be the biggest shareholder."

"The biggest? What about his father?"

"He died a couple of weeks ago, suicide. The shares went to the company itself and were pretty equally divided between the holders, it says it on here, I think that's what this file is for."

"He committed suicide?" I asked.

"He did, yeah. Didn't you hear? It was a big deal." He said it with drunk emphasis on big.

"Right, yeah, yeah. I just forgot," I said. "I had no idea Walter had shares in Donovan steel, especially this much. Must've been fucking expensive."

I pulled the paper away from Thomas' eyes to look at it again. Didn't really matter, though, I didn't understand most of what was on it.

"Wasn't Jack supposed to get the company after his father?" I asked.

"Probably, it's the most obvious," he stopped talking and looked at me. "You think he would?" He asked.

"Would what?" I asked. He made a cutting gesture at his throat.

"What, kill him?" I asked. He was my main suspect, together with Thomas. Who, I realized, was right here with me, feeding me drunk.

"Maybe," I just said. "A lot of people think you did, actually," I said. Thomas laughed and put his hand on my shoulder.

"I'm not gonna lie, if I could've, I would've. Sadly, someone else was faster," he said. He took his hand of my shoulder to pour another glass. I raised my eyebrows and grinned, though it wasn't that funny.

"I think a lot of the people that are in this house would've," I said, taking the glass from him.

"Yeah? Would you?" He asked, after which he downed the drink. I swished the whiskey around in the glass.

"Probably, he was a bit of an ass," I said. And I did, in a way. I wrote him to die. Who's the real villain here, me or the person who physically killed him?

"He was, wasn't he? Quite an unpleasant fellow." He put the glass back and rested his hands behind him on the desk, slightly leaning back. He tilted his head and looked at me.

"Yeah, I heard about your property," I started and downed the drink. "I could help you out, if you need anything." I put the glass down and grimaced from the liver damage I could feel coming up for when I would turn 70. He waved it away.

"It's alright, maybe I'm not meant to be a baker."

"Yeah you are," I said. "You're really good at it." He looked me in the eyes and smiled. I put my hand on his shoulder and smiled back. His shoulder was warm, as was my hand. Blood was pumping through us crazy fast with all the alcohol that we pumped into ourselves.

I left my hand sit just a little too long. Thomas didn't move it. Neither did we break eye contact. My brain sort of did, blurring my vision as it always did when I got drunk. I slid my hand down his arm and pulled it away. I didn't know if it was the alcohol or whatever it was but I felt a little something. I coughed.

"Ah, you know what I mean," I said.

"No, thank you. I appreciate it," he said.

We sat there for a couple of seconds, kind of awkward. It didn't *feel* awkward. I wondered. I reached for his face. He didn't flinch or move away. He just looked at me. I didn't need anything more. Fuck, what the fuck. I grabbed his jaw, he *kept* looking. He was the only thing not blurry. I led his face closer.

"Yeah?" I asked.

"Yeah," he replied.

Without another second of hesitation I pulled his face to mine and dove into his lips. He dove equally as quick. A rush went to my head and I felt myself turn blood red. I grasped his thigh. He tasted like cake and alcohol. My heart beat faster and faster, I could feel his do the same. He buried his hand in my hair and pulled just a little bit. I couldn't stop. I didn't want to. He was married. I knew he was. I reached further up his thigh and grabbed the back of his neck with my other hand. Strong neck. The world was spinning around us. I didn't know if it was the alcohol or the moment. Probably the first. His free hand grabbed my hand, the one up his thigh, and led it even closer to him.

"Are you sure?" I asked in between lips.
"Give me your little Nardo," he said. Jesus. I knew that'd come back somehow. I pulled away, attempting to look annoyed, but I couldn't help but grin.
"Well don't stop *now*," he said.

He pulled me in again. Who knew cake and alcohol were such a good mix. He stood up without breaking contact and rested his hands on my hips. I traced his back and reached his ass. I grinned. His head went down and I felt the button that held my pants up loosen. I barely saw him, room still blurred. I reached for his head and stroked his hair. I leaned back on the desk. What was this story turning into?

The smell of smoke dissipated slowly because of the open door but didn't leave completely, probably burned into the furniture and walls of the study. We were hanging back on the couch. Still far from sober.
"If it means anything, I think you're bigger than Jack," Thomas said. I laughed.
"Ah thank you," I said.

"You know what, I'm feeling like having a cocktail, I don't think I've even had one today," he said. I pulled a shocked face.

"You gotta," I said. I stood up, holding the arm of the couch to keep my balance and held out my hand to Thomas. His warm, slightly sweaty hand grabbed mine and he pulled himself up from the desk.

"I gotta," he said and we started walking, hands held to not fall over. Out the door we went, closing it behind us.

"Nancy made them, you know," Thomas said.

"Then we gotta even more," I replied. I felt a little weird hearing Nancy's name but the feeling passed as quickly as it came. We stumbled trough the hallway with the weird paintings. Thomas pointed at one and laughed.

"That's you," he said. It was a painting of a monkey with a top-hat, standing next to a demon of some sort. I laughed too.

"And you," I said.

We walked on, towards the roses. I picked one and gave it to Thomas, who smiled giddily. We tried walking the stairs but skipped more than we used, sort of half gliding, half walking from the stairs. We held onto each other for dear life, pulling each other down the stairs until we reached the bottom of it. I looked at him the same time he looked at me and we both burst out in laughter. Gasping for breath Thomas gestured to the sitting area.

"Cocktail," he managed to get out.

"Right!" I laughed. He took my hand and we walked into the room, through the big archway.

Thomas and I stumbled into the room and sat down on the couch, still holding hands. Marilyn raised her eyebrow.

"You got any cocktails left?" Thomas asked.

"I'd say you've had a few," Marilyn answered. Thomas and I looked at each other and grinned. No tail, though.

"Don't just sit there with those smug grins, what have you two been up to?"

"Whiskey, best one I've had in years," I said. Marilyn's face changed from the raised eyebrow to a concerned face.

"From upstairs? You didn't take it from my father did you?" She asked. Thomas grinned even more.

"He won't be drinking it anymore, so I figured we might. Would be a shame to waste it, right?" Marilyn looked up to the ceiling and closed her eyes in what I assume was annoyance.

"It's been just hours since he died, Thom. Please, you knobhead."

"Was worth it," he said.

Jack and Samuel came and sat closer to us so they could join in the conversation.

"Without me?" Jack said. Thomas and I shot him our best sorry looks.

"You weren't questioned yet," Thomas said. "We can go back after."

"Yeah, man, we'll gladly have you," I said.

"You would? I thought you didn't like him?" Marilyn asked.

"Don't be so closed minded," I said. "Besides, he's a nice looking guy." Jack and Thomas both laughed. Marilyn didn't, she looked confused as hell. I waved it away with my hand.

"He's alright."

"Is it the drunk in you speaking or do you actually think so?" She asked.

"I think a bit of both."

The door of the room on the side of the sitting area once again opened and revealed Joan.

"Nardo just said he loves me," Jack said to her. He probably had a few drinks with Samuel too. Joan looked surprised.

"That's great, honey," she said. "Scott asks if you would come in, though."

"Alright, see the lot of you later," Jack said. He stood up and walked to the office.

"Good luck," I said.

Joan walked over to us, giving Jack a kiss on the cheek on the way over.

"Can I talk to you, Nardo?" She asked. "In private?"

Chapter five

"Yeah, where do you wanna go?" I replied.

"What's wrong?" Marilyn asked before Joan could say anything back.

"Oh, nothing's *wrong*, really. I just want to have a chat with him," she then turned back to me. "Let's go to the kitchen, okay?" She said. I stood up, holding the back of the couch to not fall over right away. Joan frowned,

"You're drunk?" She said. I nodded.

"That explains the love-confession with Jack," she said. She walked over to me and gave her arm as support.

The kitchen was even bigger than the sitting area, with the family room attached to it, same with the breakfast room. Stairs led from beside the breakfast room to upstairs and a big kitchen isle stood in the centre of the kitchen. The kitchen itself was very big, as if it served a restaurant rather than just one family. Some of the food Nancy had prepared stood out on the kitchen top, together with more drinks. It looked like she had prepared the food yesterday in advance for today. Since she was the only maid present today, that was probably a great idea.

The seats in the breakfast room were a blue type of velvet, and Joan and I sat down in them. They were really soft. Felt a bit like a nice blanket. I stretched and slouched down in it to make me touch as much of it as possible. It felt like I was getting a hug from a big teddybear. I groaned in happiness. It was dark in the room, the only light coming from the creek in the doors leading to the kitchen.

"What's up?" I asked. She seemed to hesitate.
"I know you said you suspected me and I you, but I want to ask you to put that aside for a few minutes," she said. I nodded.
"I didn't actually suspect you," I said. She frowned.
"Why did you say so, then?"
"Because you looked at me when someone asked who you thought it was."
"Well—," she said. I waved it away.
"Don't worry, silly. You're all good." She smiled a little. I pointed at it and smiled back.
"There it is, I love that smile," I said. I leaned back into the seat even more and stared at her, smiling. She started blushing. It's been a while since I saw her do that, for me at least.
"I don't suspect you to be the murderer either," she said, "not anymore, at least—," I interrupted her.
"Good! Lovely!" I said.
"But Scott said you told him Nancy had pills in her room, he thought they might be poison. Did he tell you?" See, he suspected Thomas to be the murderer. Same as in the original story. I tried to look surprised. I probably looked like a cartoon doing it.
"Ooh no, the pills? Really?" I asked. Joan nodded.
"He does." I sat for a second and tried to clear my head. I felt a little nauseous.
"Okay, what do we do now?" I asked.
"Well, next he has to examine the crime scene a bit more with the new information he has gathered and then he wants to see the pills. Do you really think Nancy did it?"
"Noo, not Nancy. She's as sweet as honey. She doesn't look like a killer." Joan laughed softly.

"None of them do, they're all drunk."

"You're not," I said. "Not a lot, at least." She sighed and looked at one of the books on the table, then back at me. Her blonde hair glowed gold in the soft light.

"You're pretty," I said. She looked a little taken aback.

"Just an observation, don't worry," I said. I yawned. "Sorry, I'm drunk."

"I can tell. I can't drink in situations like these. He may not have been my favorite person but he is family," she said. I nodded slowly.

"He wasn't mine either. I don't think he was anyone's."

"I think he might be Mari's favorite. Did you see how she cried when we found his body?"

"And you didn't," I said.

"No, I didn't."

"You cold, cold woman," I said, semi old-vagabond like. She acted as if she hadn't heard it. Fine.

"Why do you want my opinion?" I asked.

"Hm?"

"Mine, of all people. You thought I did it."

"Because you told Scott about the pills," she said.

"Could be fake. Maybe I wanted to throw him off."

"I doubt that."

"You wanna see them?"

"what— now?" She asked. I stood up, grabbed her hand and pulled her on her feet too. Just a second later I grabbed her by her shoulder not to fall over.

"Sorry," I said, then regained my stability and led her to the stairs.

The door swung open once more. I swung out my arm to say she could take the lead — not that she wasn't already. The light flicked on and the sweet scent of whatever type of perfume it was hit my nose again. I could almost put my finger on the smell this time. So close.

63

"Which one is it," Joan asked, who was already in the room.

"The one with the cap," I said. Joan groaned.

"Don't drink next time," she said. "All of them have caps." I walked over and gave her the one. Click clacking on the ground with my fancy shoes. Even Joan with her high heels was less bad.

"That's the one," I said, pointing to it when she took it.

"You're welcome." She unscrewed the cap and looked at it. She hummed.

"Well?"

"No clue."

"Then why did you want to see them?"

"You took me with you, I don't know the differences in pills," she said.

"You're not of much use, are you?"

"You sound like my uncle," she said.

"Don't kill me next time, love," I replied. She put the bottle down and slapped me in the face. I froze. Didn't move my facial expression, didn't move anything. My drunk brain barely processed what the fuck happened.

"Don't do that," she said and walked out of the room.

"What the fuck did I do?" I asked while following her out. She stopped and turned to me.

"You don't get to say things like that. You don't know anything about me." She started walking again.

"What is there to know?" I said, stupidly.

She turned around a last time, angry face, and reached for her foot. She took off her shoe and before I could even think about how ugly she actually looked when she was angry, the shoe flew to my head. I hit my shoulder, actually hurting more than you'd think based on how hard you imagine a woman like Joan would throw. She turned around and stormed off. Fuck that. Now when I finally got friendly with Jack I somehow pissed off Joan.

I sat down on the ground and picked up Joans heel. Silver and shiny. I brought it closer. Not as clean as it looked from farther away. Just like her personality. Fucking bitch. Finally a sliver of Jessica came out. Thank god I didn't have to put up with that in real life anymore. I'd rather murder *myself* than dealing with that shit again.

I picked on the sole. Wasn't clean either. Some white ish sticker was stuck on it. It wasn't as white as it probably was before, obviously walked on. Even though it was in the state it was in, I could sort of read what it said. "Ginedair's" in antique letters.
"Huh, gin," I murmured. "Yeah." I stood up, crouching against the wall and started walking downstairs, for, you guessed it, gin. I left the shoe on the ground. Fuck that shoe. If she needed it, she wouldn't have thrown it.

I walked back into the sitting room. Thomas and Samuel were playing the card game Jack and Samuel were playing before and Marilyn was surprisingly talking to Jack. It didn't seem to be a good talk, both very visibly annoyed at each other.
"Jack?" I said. I didn't think he'd be out already. Scott wasn't out yet, though. He looked up and nodded a greeting.
"Ah, Nardo, right in time." He said and scooted away from Marilyn. He patted on the seat next to him as to gesture to sit with him.
"Is Scott not done?" I asked, and sat down on the chair he patted on.
"Studying his findings, I believe. He told me it would just take a moment," Jack said.

65

"How did it go anyway?" Samuel asked, joined in the conversation.

"He's a nice guy but his questions were a tad unusual," Jack answered. "He asked me what my biggest fear was." Samuel clapped in his hands and pointed at Jack.

"Right! It's weird!" He exclaimed. He threw a card on the table and grabbed his glass. "Why would he ask that?"

"To get into your mind," I said. Thomas nodded but didn't look away from his cards.

"I liked his method. It's one of the reasons he always solves his cases. He gets into his suspects' heads to see their motives." He looked up and grinned.

"Though I think with Marilyn he got into something else than her head." She replied with a content smile.

"He did," she said.

"Say, Nardo, where is Joan?" Jack asked.

"I honestly don't know, I thought she went back here."

"Maybe she's fixing her face," Samuel suggested.

"Ah, perhaps," Jack said, and that was that.

"Do you have gin left?" I asked. Jack nodded.

"In the kitchen, I believe. Come to think of it, Nancy still hasn't brought me that drink," he said.

"Yes, I'll check on her in a second," Thomas said. Joan walked in, ignored me and sat down next to Jack, who she gave a little kiss.

"Hey, darling," Jack said.

He had barely finished his sentence when the door swung open. Scott walked out with a face that again gave nothing away. Of course, he had close to no alcohol in his system and was doing his job, but I still found it very impressive. He walked up to us and stood at the front of the area.

"Thank you all for cooperating. The following time will be used to examine the information I've gathered about certain things I believe to be clues as to who and what is the cause of the tragedy that happened earlier today," he paused. "I advise you to get some rest for the time being if you feel fatigued in any way, since I believe this night won't be over anytime soon. It may seem quite obvious, but I want to ask you to stay inside in any case since leaving is considered to be fleeing the scene and won't be taken lightly. Does anyone have any questions for now?"

He spoke with the same authority he had in the office but managed to sound kind despite it. I wrote him so well. No one said anything. Scott nodded.
"Very well, I will start by taking another look at the departed mister Stonier, has anyone been near him that I should know of?" There was a humming of 'no'.
"Good," he said and walked out.

"Do you guys want to join in?" Samuel said, pointing to the card game.
"No thank you, I remember what it's like playing with you," Jack said. Samuel grinned.
"I always win," he said.
"Cheat, you mean." Jack drank the last of his drink and put the glass down.
"Come to think of it, you *do* have an awful lot of 'luck'," Thomas said.
"I'm a very lucky guy," Samuel said. Joan stood up from the couch.
"I'm going to the bathroom, so count me out," she said.
"Gone again," Marilyn sighed. "I'll miss you."
"You think you'll manage on your own or do you want me to come along?" Jack asked. Joan rolled her eyes with a grin and walked away.

"Alright. Nardo? Are you in?" Samuel asked.

"I'll join the next round," I said.

"Suit yourself," Samuel said and looked back at his cards.

The second soul-crumbling scream of the night filled the air, this time coming from Joan. All of our heads jerked in the same direction. Jack jumped up and ran in the direction of the scream.

"What the hell was that?" Marilyn asked.

"Another scream? Are you kidding? I'm not drunk enough for this," Samuel said. With that sentence, the realization hit both Thomas and me and he bolted out of the room. Nancy. Fucking hell, Nancy. I forgot about her.

I heard Joan and the others mumble and yell in the kitchen. It felt like my skin was dripping. Samuel and I looked at each other, both concerned.

"Do we want to see this?" He asked.

"No, we don't," I replied.

"Can we in good consciousness stay here?" Samuel followed up.

"I don't think we can," I said. Samuel sighed and defeatedly threw his cards on the table.

"Would it hurt ya to lie?" he asked. We stood up and walked into the kitchen. Before I even set foot in it I heard Thomas yell an even more crushing scream. That one really got through to my soul.

The group of people stood around the bathroom, all with hands in front of their mouths in pure shock or on the shoulders of Thomas, who sat on his knees next to Nancy's lifeless body. On the toilet she sat, leaning against the wall, motionless, with her eyes staring dead into my soul. Her pupils looked very open, like she'd been scared to death or high as balls on drugs.

"Fuck," I said. The sight of her dead body was gruesome. I had seen the count dead before, but his eyes had already been closed by Scott. He didn't look me right in the eyes with his dead, lifeless eyes. There wasn't a more accurate picture of 'the consequences of your actions staring you in the face'. My attention flicked from her to Thomas and back at her. Thomas' cries carried throughout the house and through my body. He grasped at Nancy as if he tried to keep her soul from leaving, though as far as I could tell, it had left at least an hour ago. God, that meant Joan and I had been in the same room as a dead body. An undiscovered one, I mean.

Scott came in with a bit of a jog. I saw his face visibly turn shocked as he walked into the bathroom. He placed a hand on Thomas' shoulder and closed his eyes for a moment. Jack and Joan were in a hug, Joan too upset to look at Nancy for any longer. She was crying. Jack just stood there with a pale face, holding Joan. I put my hand on Marilyn's shoulder, she put hers on top of mine. She was shaking a little bit, but she wasn't crying like she was with her father.

"Can I?" Scott asked Thomas, gesturing he wanted to check if she was actually dead. She was, I could once again tell him that much. So far the story was still on schedule, at least one good thing about this shit. Thomas didn't reply, holding Nancy's hand while looking at the floor with his eyes closed. Scott put his fingers on Nancy's neck to check for pulse.
"She's gone," he said. Thomas let out another helpless scream and I heard Joan make the same noise, just a little softer. Jack stroked her hair and still didn't say anything. I felt an urge to do the same with Thomas. I didn't. It was

69

like I was stapled to the ground. I felt guilty. I felt like I
didn't belong there.

"God rest her soul," Samuel mumbled.

"I'm so sorry, Thomas," I said. He was still holding Nancy.
What was even worse than seeing Nancy dead was seeing
Thomas like this. I couldn't do shit. I already wrote it.

"It's best to get back to the other area, let's give him some
privacy," Scott said. Marilyn took my hand and directed
me with her out of the room. Jack and Joan followed and
Samuel shuffled after them, throwing a few last glances at
Nancy and Thomas. Scott closed the door behind us.

We all sat down silently, not knowing what to say. What
was there to say? The music that was playing was the only
sound in the room, besides Thomas' cries coming from the
kitchen.

There were no provoking questions from Marilyn, no
drunk remarks from Samuel, no comments from jack and
no shoes from Joan.

Samuel slowly grabbed a glass of alcohol that Nancy had
made, brought it to his lips and paused. He put it back on
the table with the other glasses without drinking anything.

"Samuel not drinking, there truly is something going on,"
Marilyn said. There it was, provoking. She wasn't wrong,
though. It took much for Sam not to drink.

"Oh, curse you, Marilyn," Samuel replied.

"I'm just saying," she said and leaned back in her chair.

"That's the problem, you should stop speaking," Jack said.
"All you speak is crap."

The door of the kitchen opened and Scott stuck his head
out.

"I'm about to carry her outside to the balcony, could
someone open the door?" He asked. I nodded and walked
to the door of the hallway leading to the balcony. I

70

couldn't see straight yet but at least I could walk like I could. It almost felt like I was sort of sobering up. Maybe the adrenaline. I opened the door and walked into the hallway to open the doors of the balcony.

The carpet was still a little wet from the snow outside that had blown in when we found out the count died. It was a little bit like walking on wet grass. All you can do is hope your socks won't get wet through your shoes. I opened the door and stepped onto the balcony. The cold air hit me like a brick. My vision cleared the fuck up for a second, not long enough to feel normal again but long enough to see outside. It was very beautiful, the view, but I was glad I at least chose a period in time they had some type of heating system.

The count was still laying the same way he was before — would be weird if he wasn't. I couldn't bring up any sympathy for him, I didn't feel sorry for killing him off. There were specks of ice forming on him, he looked even more dead than when I arrived. Jack and Scott walked out of the house, carrying Nancy. For her I felt more sympathy. Even though I didn't know her that well, she didn't deserve to die.

"Could you spread out the blanket on the ground, Berratare?" Scott asked me while walking onto the balcony, nodding with his head to the blanket on his shoulder.
"Yeah, of course," I said. The old guy, however, was laying straight on the tiles. I put down the blanket and put the other half on top of Nancy after Jack and Scott put her on it. After a look back at Nancy and the count we walked back inside, away from the cold. Thank god for that, a

little longer out there in my apparently not-that-thick suit would make me look the same as Stonier.

Scott closed the door and blew into his hands.

"It's a bit chilly," he said.

"It's freezing, mate, I nearly froze my dick off out there," Jack said.

"Do you know what killed Nancy?" I asked Scott. I wanted to get straight to the point before I lost my couple of seconds of soberness.

"Not quite yet, it's hard to say without an autopsy from someone who studied this specific field. I know the basic workings but I'm no use past a certain point. It might be poison but it might very well have been a heart-attack," he said. "We'll only be certain in the morrow when we can take the two to a morgue."

"It's crazy, two deaths in one evening. It can hardly be an accident," Jack said.

"Perhaps, but it's happened before. Heart-attacks are not uncommon," Scott said. "It's unfortunate we couldn't examine her sooner like we could mister Stonier, it might have given us a clearer diagnosis."

"Imagine how long she sat there," I said.

"No thanks," Jack replied.

"I hope to find the culprit this evening. When the storm calms and the roads are back in service, there is a chance they might disappear," Scott said.

"Who, the heart attacks?" Jack asked. Scott smiled a polite smile.

"I haven't said it's my opinion that the cause is a heart attack. No matter, I'm going to try and put everyone at ease as much as I can, panic is the last thing we need," Scott said.

He walked back into the sitting room, leaving me and Jack.

"Do you buy it?" He asked. "A heart-attack?" I shrugged. I didn't know. It'd be lazy writing, but again, I got kind of lazy after few pages.

"It would be weird, two deaths in one night, if only one would be a murder," I said.

"It's 50/50 but I would bet Nancy's death was a murder too."

"Maybe. Let's get back to the other room, this cold is fucking lethal." He nodded and we walked back into the room. He sat down next to Joan and put his arm around her. Samuel still didn't drink any of the alcohol on the table.

"What's gonna happen next?" He asked. I could tell he was sobering up a bit, he looked clearer out of his eyes than he did before.

"Well, it has become more complex. We haven't found the culprit from the first murder yet, this new death complicates things," Scott said.

"So you don't know, is what you're saying," Samuel replied.

"Let him speak, Samuel," Marilyn said.

"However," Scott continued, not bothered by Samuel, "There is one aspect in the investigation that might connect the two deaths." He probably meant the pills, the ones I found in Nancy's room, the ones Joan didn't know either. Maybe Scott knew what they were, he's probably seen thousands of different types of pills and poisons through his work. I doubted it were cat-pills like Marilyn thought. Her cat wasn't even here.

"Do you mind?" He asked me.

"What is it?" Samuel asked.

"I'm afraid I can't say," Scott replied.

73

"And I'm afraid to die, you son of a bitch. The least you can do is give us some truth," Samuel said.

"I understand your concern, but this is not arguable. Now, Leonardo?"

"No, I'll gladly show you," I said. "Do you want me to take you now?" Scott smiled and swiftly turned to Jack.

"Would you make sure Thomas gets into the sitting area? Staying at the place his wife passed away in for too long will make the process of grief harder to start."

"Of course, I'll get to him," Jack said. He stroked Joans hair, gave her a kiss and walked towards the kitchen. Scott turned back to me.

"Lead the way," he said and nodded towards the hallway.

Once again I climbed the huge stairs, past the big pots of roses, one of the roses from them still laying on the table in the sitting area where Thomas put it after I gave it to him. I felt the drunkness return a little bit. Shouldn't have had that much whiskey, sure, but when do you get another chance to taste a vintage like this? A vintage in a vintage time, meaning it's one that was probably a hundred years older than I was — *at least*.

Scott's steps were quiet as hell compared to my click-clacking dress shoes. He looked good in his suit, better than I did in mine. I never wore one, he wore them everyday. We walked past the painting of the baby with the dog-lollipop in front of the maze and arrived at Nancy's room. Scott gestured me to open the door.

"Please, do the honors" he said. The room was as dark as before. The air of perfume still hung around as strong as it was before. It made me think of Marilyn, probably stuck in my brain from earlier. Some type of memory trigger. Now I

74

was here with her date. Weird turn of events. I flicked on the light and waited for Scott to walk in. He sniffed.

"Perfume," I said.

"Indeed," he said. I saw his eyes flick through the room, probably deducting clues from what he could see so far. "Would you mind showing me the pills?"

"Right," I said. I walked towards the desk with the stacks of books and the fuck ton of bottles of who knows what. Maybe they had pills too, even more poisonous than the ones I saw earlier. Maybe they *were* for her cat.

I wondered how mine was doing, he was in the room when I fell. I read somewhere that if you're dead for a few days, they will start eating you because they have no other food. Was my cat eating me?

I looked back at Scott, who patiently looked back at me. I looked back at the desk and almost immediately saw the one Joan put back on there before she slapped me. A quick flash of Marilyn's outreached hand came through to my brain at the same time. The last thing I should probably do was think about Marilyn now, her detective-date was right here with me. Fuck, what if he could tell? I straightened out my face and picked up the bottle. Just think about Joan. Instant anti boner. I gave it to Scott and leaned back on the desk. He took the lid off of the bottle and put it on the desk, as I had before. With a nice flick of the wrist he shook the bottle lightly and looked focused. He took one pill out and smelled it, then held it out for me to smell too.

The light brown, a bit yellowish pill was even smaller in comparison to Scotts hand.

"Odorless," he stated. No smell. Why the hell did he let me smell anyway, then? I couldn't smell it. Though I don't think I could tell even if there was a smell thanks to the amount of perfume in the room. I nodded.

"Do you know what it is?" I asked. Scott bit his lip and flipped the pill over with his finger.

"It could be a range of types of pills, perhaps oxytocin. It isn't widely available so it's hard to believe she had access to it," he pondered. "Maybe Senna Glycoside or Quinine, though I can't find a reason for either to be of use for her." I had no idea what any of those pills were. Wasn't glycoside sugar? I'm kidding, I know it's not. But I didn't know what it meant, I should've done more research on common pills back in this time.

"She didn't have any type of illness, did she?" He asked.

"Thomas would know, but I don't," I replied. Scott's eyes darted trough the room again.

"Perhaps we can find a reference as to what the pills may be in the room, would you be so kind to look in the bathroom? I will investigate the room we're currently in," he said. The bathroom? What the fuck would I find in the bathroom? Soap? What, she killed the count — or herself — with soap?

"Sure," I said. Scott smiled gratefully and started searching for whatever it was that he was looking for. I sighed and opened the bathroom door.

An even bigger waft of perfume hit me in the face when I walked into the bathroom. In a reflex I turned my face away and blinked a couple of times. Even Jessica didn't use *this* much perfume. I coughed and waved my hand in front of my nose and mouth to try and get the smell away. Was there no ventilation here or what?

"Fuck," I murmured.

The bathroom was, as everything in this house, bigger than mine. I'd say it was pretty stylish for it's time but it

76

looked very old-fashioned. I think my grandma had one of these walls, white stones combined with those flower vine tiles as division every meter or so. Silver looking taps and shower head, though they were probably steel because it was a maid's bathroom, not a Stonier's. A towel closet on the left of the door, made of some dark type of wood with flower type decorations. It looked pretty expensive, though I doubt it was. She didn't make *that* much by being a maid. Neither did Thomas with his bakery.

I opened one of the doors to look inside of it. Some pink towels, a few sponges, but no clues of what the pills could be. As expected. I walked over to the mirror and sink. There was a sponge on it, which was dried up, but I could see the imprint of water that had leaked out of it in the sink. She'd probably used it a little over a day ago. Look at me, deducting useless shit.

I picked it up and just looked at it for a few seconds. Scott would probably want me to try my best, meaning I'd have to stay in here for a while to 'investigate'. Great sponge, pretty good quality. Maybe she could stick it down the count's throat and kill him by suffocation. I scoffed and laid it back down.

There was a vase next to the mirror, though there wasn't anything in it. In the abundance of flowers in the bathroom's decoration, a vase was the one place there weren't any. It wasn't a very nice looking vase, though. It looked more like a glass bottle than anything. Maybe she was an alcoholic, like Samuel. I highly doubted it. I looked up a little. Oh, wow. One of the best looking things in the room. I smiled at it. My reflection smiled back.

I went with my hand trough my hair. I felt a thread of the suit tickle me. It was weird, wearing someone else's clothes. I could hear Scott still tearing up the room next to me, obviously having more material to work with than I did. I sighed once more and turned to the bathtub. A couple of vials and soap bars were in the open cabinet next to it. I didn't know if soap in this time was poisonous or not, but I doubted she could kill someone with it. Most she could do was make them smell good. Which, judging the amount of perfume in there, she was into.

I mindlessly opened one of the vials and immediately regretted it. The strong prickly smell made my eyes water and hurt my nose. I instantly got sober.
"Ah, fuck," I mumbled. "Jesus christ."

Chapter six

I closed the vial as fast as I could. It was one of the strongest things I've ever smelled. Who the hell would voluntarily use it? Had to be a psycho of some sort. No one could attract people with this shit. It would repel them. Nasty ass shit.

Scott opened the door and raised his eyebrows when the perfume hit him.
"Have you found anything?" he asked. I rubbed my eyes and sniffed.
"Women's stuff," I said.
"And even more perfume." Scott said, looking thoughtful. He had a quick look around the bathroom, but his face didn't give anything away.
"Good observation," I said. "Have you found anything in the room?"
"Not quite, the loose papers are mostly studies of different languages and there weren't any other possible clues to be found in the room, besides the excessive use of perfume."
"Can you read any of it?" I asked.
"Some of it, yes. Not quite all. But I did not find out any more than we already knew."
"Maybe she tried to cover something up with the perfume," I suggested and handed him the vial of awful smelling whatever-it-was. He took it, opened it, smelled it and closed it as fast as I had. His face didn't change, he didn't even blink. How the fuck did he do that.
"Camphor. You might be right, it is very possible the perfume is a tool to mask it. But to what end?" He said. To what end indeed. He worded it beautifully.

"Have you found anything else in here?" He asked me. A newfound love for elegant wording, indeed.

"I don't think so, it looked normal to me. Have you?" He didn't immediately reply, looking around the room another time, more carefully than last time. His gaze fell on the sink with the sponge.

"I might know what the pills are," he said.

"What?" I asked.

"Poor Nancy," he mumbled.

"What is it?"

"Quinine, most commonly used as a cure for malaria, but less known is that together with the sponge, camphor and the glass bottle it's used in make-shift home-abortions. Meaning—," he said. Oh, fucking hell.

"She was pregnant," I continued. He nodded. I killed off a pregnant woman. Or, rather, a former pregnant woman. Neither the kid nor the woman were alive now. Double homicide. Worse, I fucked a soon-to-be-dad.

"Camphor is a numbing-agent."

"A numbing agent?"

"It numbs the area one applies it to."

"Jesus, was that shit that painful?"

"I will not go into details, but indeed. Most certainly."

"That's the reason she's gone wild with the perfume, then. She didn't want anyone to know," I said. Did Thomas even know?

"Likely. This might even solve her death," Scott said.

"Really?" I asked.

Groundbreaking shit, for the story at least. I never knew what her death was, I hadn't reached the end of my book yet. In the original story, Scott didn't even know what did it at the point I stopped writing. Me being here must've

80

stirred up some shit. Didn't know if that was bad or good for myself but a breakthrough is a breakthrough.

"The quinine pills. She has likely overdosed on them. She came across as confused before. Her pupils were dilated, which might be a sign of retinal intoxication. She could've been blind — or going blind— for the last couple of hours she was alive."
"*Blind?*" I asked. That's why she didn't look at any of us. Jesus, that wasn't what I signed up for. I didn't want her to suffer.
Scott put the vial of camphor in his pocket, where I could tell by the rounding of it, the bottle of quinine was in too. "I'm going to take these as evidence," he explained.
"I'm not doubting you," I replied.

Once again I closed the door to Nancy's room. This time with Scott instead of Marilyn. Didn't feel the same amount of attraction, but it was close. We silently walked trough the hallway. The huge, huge hallway.

"How do you think Thomas will take it?" I asked.
"It depends on whether he knew she was pregnant or not."

Right, she did the abortion probably knowing the risk of it. She essentially would've rather died than had the baby. Man, this story was dark. How did my subconscious come up with this shit? I rubbed my eyes with one hand and refocused. I wasn't fully sober yet. I kind of felt like I was dozing off.

"We know it wasn't the same method as the count, though," I said. "That's progress."
"Indeed. This eliminates a considerable amount of questions, yet raises some too." Like why the fuck she used

a home abortion. To be fair, I didn't know if abortions were allowed in this time, but even then.

"Hey Nardo," Jack greeted. He nodded to Scott. Thomas sat next to him on the couch, elbows on his knees, leaning forward. Staring into nothing with a blank face and dead eyes. Not as dead as his wife's, but sad to see nonetheless.
"Hey Jack," I said as I sat next to Marilyn on the couch on the opposite side of Jack and Thomas. Joan sat in one of the chairs, still seeming genuinely upset.
"So, what's the news?" Jack said semi-smiling, though I could see that he was fucked up about this shit. I looked at Scott, waiting for what he would do. He seemed to hesitate a little.
"We found some considerable evidence," he started, but fell silent for a little bit. Marilyn raised her eyebrows.
"Well?" She said. "What is it?" Thomas turned up to Scott and looked at him blankly.
"About Nancy?" He asked. Scott nodded slowly.
"About Nancy."
"What did you find?" Thomas asked.
"We found the culprit of her passing away," he said. Shocked gasps filled the room.
"Quinine pills, camphor, a sponge and a glass bottle." Thomas looked confused, but Joan's face lit up in recognition.
"No," she stammered. "Are you sure?" Scott nodded.
"I am," he said. "It's undeniable."
"I didn't know she was—," she started.
"What is it?" Thomas asked. His blank face made place for a confused and irritated one.
"A home abortion," I said. Thomas' head jerked and his eyes spread wide open.
"I'm so sorry, mate," Jack said, putting his hand on Thomas' shoulder.

"The abortion killed her?" Marilyn asked.

"The quinine pills did, yes," Scott said. On the other side of the table was a loud bang. Thomas hit it with his fist in what was probably a wave of anger or sadness. He put his face in his hands.

"I'm terribly sorry Thomas, I am," Scott said.

"I told her to wait on the doctor," Thomas said with a near-crying, half angry voice. "I bloody told her."

"You knew she wanted to get an abortion?" Jack asked. Thomas hummed yes.

"You did?" Marilyn asked. She looked on edge. She looked like how I was feeling since I got here.

"She told me a few days ago," he answered. "But the doctor was out of town. I didn't know she was going to bloody *do it now*." Scott sat down on a chair, his pretty eyes focused on Marilyn.

"If I had known, I would've stopped her," Joan said. "Poor Nancy, it must've hurt."

"Would you, though?" Marilyn asked. I scoffed. I doubted it. Self serving bitch that Joan was.

"What's that supposed to mean?"

"Just asking."

"Then stop asking such dumb questions," Joan said.

"It's not dumb, Joan."

"Well then, Marilyn, would *you*?" Joan asked.

Marilyn didn't respond. I frowned. She did seem kinda eager to *leave* Nancy's room earlier, when we were doing our thing.

"*Would* you?" I asked, turned to her. She frowned.

"Would I stop Nancy from doing an abortion?" She asked, avoiding the actual question.

"On herself," I said. "Would you?" Everyone now looked at Marilyn.

"Marilyn?" Scott asked. "Were you aware of Mrs. Jones' abortion?" Talking in his detective voice again.

"Are you seriously asking me if I knew?" Again avoiding the question by asking another.

"I am," he said. She looked offended and looked around for support.

"Did you know?" Thomas asked repulsed.

"Why would you even ask me that?" She asked.

"Did you, Marilyn?" He asked, now angry. Marilyn looked around for support and scoffed.

"It wasn't supposed to kill her, it was supposed to only kill the goddamn baby!" She exclaimed.

That's why she wanted me to leave the room earlier, she even tried to get my attention away from the pills by — I was such a fucking idiot. I was in a murder mystery, what did I expect? For the femme fatale not to be the femme fatale? That's why she 'didn't know' the pills. Why she didn't want to split up. Dear god, was I stupid. She had the same blood as Joan.

"Marilyn, you bloody arse," Jack said. "You stupid bloody cunt."

"*I* at least tried to help. She trusted me with that information. Can you say the same? No!" Marilyn said.

"Because you were the only damn person around in the house!" Thomas yelled. "What is wrong with you? Why would you risk her life — not only risk, you took it!"

"I didn't take it!" Marilyn yelled back. "It was an *accident!*"

And it was Thomas' wife and child, may have been an accident too but at least he was trying to get her to a doctor.

84

"Let's keep order," Scott said loudly. Everybody fell quiet. The authority and respect this man had was incredible. "Now Marilyn, did you or did you not help Miss Jones in any way to perform the abortion?"

"Well not directly," she started.

"Did you or did you not supply Miss Jones with the tools to do so?" He didn't even take her into the side room. He went full Sherlock on her right in the sitting area.

"I know someone who had those pills but—," she again couldn't finish her sentence.

"That's enough. That's all we need, Marilyn," Scott said. Thomas's face grew dark and he stared at Marilyn. I'm no behavior expert but I'd say he was trying to keep himself from round-housing the fuck out of Marilyn.

"Give me the time to finish my sentence, at least!" Marilyn said.

"Are you out of your mind? You *know* how dangerous those things are," Joan said. "You're a horrible person!"

"It wasn't like I was up inside her scooping the child out," Marilyn said defensive. "She asked *me*, I didn't go up to her asking if she needed some child removing pills!"

Did I understand where she was coming from? Yes. It could've been an accident. Knowing these times it probably was. Didn't excuse that she did it, though. Especially if it's as dangerous as it is. Didn't excuse her using her 'skills' to distract me from the pills either.

"You are so full of shit," Thomas said. "Did you kill your own father too?"

"You're crossing a line," Marilyn said. "I did not kill my father."

"Right, but you *did* kill Nancy. Doesn't that cross a bloody line?" Jack said.

"I didn't kill Nancy either, jack-off."

85

"Oh, very mature," Jack said.

"You committed an indirect murder. You supplied her with the tools that enabled the death, which makes you guilty of third degree murder," Scott said. I couldn't read his face. I couldn't read Marilyn's either, they suited each other if she hadn't killed Nancy. Bet that would be a dealbreaker for Scott.

"I didn't kill her! Was I out there stabbing the girl to death? No!" Marilyn said.

"Oh curse you, Marilyn," Thomas said, after which he walked out of the room.

"You have *no* tact, none at all," Joan said to Marilyn.

"They are accusing me of killing our maid! Tact was gone long ago!"

"Maid?" Joan said. "*Maid?* You're heartless."

"That's what she was, wasn't she?"

"She stopped being a maid the moment Thomas married her. I genuinely saw her as my friend," Joan said. Marilyn didn't say anything in reply. She took an angry sip of one of the drinks Nancy made before.

I looked at the door Thomas had walked out of. Poor guy.

"Do you want me to check up on Thomas?" I volunteered. Scott just nodded.

"I hope he's okay," Jack pondered.

"Me too," Scott said. "I very much hope he's alright.

"Hey, are you okay?" I asked, walking into the library. I knew he'd be here, it was Nancy's favorite place in the house. I heard no reply. I could just barely see his figure in the dark of the huge room.

"You're here, right?" I asked. I heard a scoff.

"Yeah, I'm here." He flicked a light on for a second and then flicked it back off. I walked up to him.

"I don't know what I am," he said. "I don't *feel* anything anymore. I felt everything just a couple of minutes ago but it's gone now. Like there's *nothing*."
"I know what you mean," I said. It was silent for a few moments. I did know what he meant. I had the same thing sometimes. So much shit going on in your head that it just turns off. Then you feel nothing.

The atmosphere in the library was nice though, it smelled like old books — I'm a writer, what did you expect? Ofcourse I like the smell of books. Thomas was staring into the library with a blank look on his face.

"I'm really sorry about Nancy," I started. He sighed.
"She was the only single reason I kept in touch with my family," he said. "I loved her."
"I know."
"I can't believe she took those pills from Marilyn," Thomas said.
"I don't think she meant for it to hurt Nancy. But what she said was out of line, she should've shut the fuck up."
"I can't believe I'm one of them," he said.
"Ah, just half, right? You've got another line of family."
"Walter's genes are evil."
I took a seat next to him, on a green velvet couch in front of a huge book case. I flicked the lamp that stood next to it back on.
"All I feel is emptiness, I don't know how to go on without her. I don't even feel sadness anymore."
"You'll figure out how to go on without her, at least you know she loved you too." He nodded.
"She did," he said. I hesitated.
"Why the abortion, then?" I asked. I felt a bit awkward asking that question, I immediately regretted it. Pretty

fucking tactless too. To my surprise he didn't look offended.

"As I said, I can't believe I'm one of them."

"Your genes? You didn't want to have the baby because of your genes?" I asked, genuinely surprised.

That was a dumb fucking reason to abort. He didn't have any bad genes health wise, and if the kid would be even a little bit like him his kid would've had a good personality too.

"It's a little different than that. A little more complicated," he said.

"Is it?" I asked. He looked into the distance, rubbing his neck. He seemed numb, like he said.

"I don't know, man," he started. I raised my hands, as if I backed off.

"No pressure, don't do anything you don't feel good to do," I said. He smiled briefly.

"Did you like Walter?" He asked. I frowned.

"Liked Walter?" Fuck no. "In short, no." He squinted his eyes and nodded.

"Do me a favor, though, don't tell anyone else. It's very private, and I want to keep it like that," he said.

"Yeah, of course," I said.

He hesitated for a second.

"The child wasn't mine," Thomas said.

My eyes flew open, same with my mouth. I felt another adrenaline rush, like every time I figured out something new. *It wasn't his?* Had Nancy slept with Walter? That's fucking awful, no wonder Thomas didn't mind the abortion. Also explained why he was open to me earlier. I was his rebound. Jesus Christ.

88

"Did she sleep with your uncle?" I said, disgusted. He
shook his head.
"You got one more guess," he said.
"Who's is it, then?" I asked.
"Oh no, it is Walter's." He said.
"Did he—," I started. He nodded.
"Raped her."
"Fuck," I said. "That fucking asshole."
"She didn't even tell me at first, she only told me when
she found out she was pregnant. She wanted to keep
working here in order for us to keep the bakery. She—,"
he cut off and closed his eyes. I didn't know what to say. I
wasn't the rebound, that much was clear. What the fuck. I
leaned my head back on the back of the couch and sighed.
"What the fuck," I said.
"I understand now why my dad didn't want anything to do
with his family," Thomas agreed.
"Oh right, you were the lost relative," I said. He frowned.
"Lost relative?" I waved it away.
"It does give you a motive, but I wouldn't blame you. I
probably would've killed the guy if he did those things to
me too," I said.
"Well, thank you, but sadly I didn't. Neither did Nancy, I
think," he paused for a while. "It's weird, I feel like she'll
walk in any moment, like nothing happened. Like she's
still here."
"Maybe that's why you feel numb, because it hasn't hit you
yet." He bit his lip.
"Not looking forward to the moment it hits. Especially
here in the library. It feels like all of it didn't happen. You
know what I mean?" He said. I did, I'd been feeling it the
entire time I was here. It happened, but it didn't. I just
nodded, giving us another silent moment.

I honestly couldn't believe some of the things that started happening. How could I not have known some of these things? I bloody wrote the book, there was more I didn't know than I did. This story actually kind of made sense in this version, I understood why some characters would kill the count. This storyline with the count raping Nancy was way beyond fucked up, it made way more sense to kill for than for a bakery. She was the one thing he cared most about.

"If there's anything I can do," I said.
"Don't worry, I'll get you immediately if there is," he replied smiling. He inhaled deeply and then looked at me. "Thank you for coming here," he said. "It genuinely means a lot."
"Yeah, of course. I know how much she meant to you. Can't let you go through that shit alone." He closed his eyes and leaned his head back.
"Do you want me to leave you alone for a moment?" I asked. He rubbed his forehead sighed.
"I don't know, I don't mind you being here. I just don't want to see Marilyn. Maybe ever, I don't think I can forgive her for what she did."
"Right, I feel you. And you don't have to, you've got every right for it," I said.
"Yeah, that's the problem. I got every right by being a Stonier. And so do they. They can get away with anything, and so can I. I'm regretting getting my father's letter more and more every day. I liked being a Jones more."
"I suppose, but it's also how you were allowed to marry Nancy, right?" I said.
"I wish she wouldn't have worked here, it would've stopped that shit-stain of a human from ever touching her. I can't bear the thought of it. It's horrible. I think that's why I'm feeling like this, I'm trying not to think about it."

He was a good self-analyst, I had to give it to him. Maybe he could analyze me next, figure out how I'm still here. "Maybe you should, maybe it'll help with the process of grief. Do you remember what Scott said? He wanted you out of the kitchen so the process of grief would start. Maybe he was wrong, maybe it's exactly where you need to be." He didn't respond.

"I'll go with you if you want, I imagine it's hard as it is, let alone going back. We can even get some whiskey to try and make it less bad the first time," I suggested. He sighed.

"I don't know Nardo, don't you think it's too early?"

"Do you?"

"Maybe. I don't know." He paused. "Maybe you're right. She's not in there anymore anyway." I nodded.

"And if you want to leave, we'll just leave and go elsewhere."

We walked through the archway to the kitchen. It was silent in there, Marilyn and Joan's chatter vaguely coming through the door at the other side of the room. I heard Thomas' breathing become more and more inconsistent the further we walked into the kitchen.

"Do you want to take a step back and go into the breakfast room instead?" I asked.

"I don't think I can do this," he said, almost looking like he was getting a panic attack. "I can't do this, I can't. It's—," He held my shoulder trying to recenter himself and faced the other way. I could feel his hand shake.

"Can we get a drink instead?" He asked. He seemed genuinely fucked up, though he was trying to keep it together. "I don't want to go there yet."

"Yeah, of course, we'll get a drink first," I replied. "And if you don't want to come back after, we won't." I nodded towards the door and started walking, his hand still on my shoulder.

I threw one last look at the toilet. It was a bad death, dark as hell. The door was closed, but the inside of it was still burned into my memory. Especially her eyes, staring into my soul. Couldn't imagine what Thomas felt. The tiles in front of the door, next to a kitchen cabinet, looked like Nancy tried to clean up some blood, which would make sense with a failed abortion. A blue dot caught my eye. I stopped walking.

"Can you wait for a second? I wanna look at something real quick," I said to Thomas. It looked almost like a button from where I was standing, from a jacket or something of the like. I walked closer and picked it up. Close, it was a cufflink. The thing on someone's shirt, a lot of people who wear suits or whatever have them. You know, the thing a lot of people lose in murder mysteries. "No," Thomas said and stepped out the door. He stopped right after, probably just needed to get out of the room. I couldn't see him, his back was against the wall. "Alright, just wait there then," I said.

I looked back at the blue thing. It had two tiny S's on it, it looked pretty expensive. Two S's? Samuel, Samuel Singretti. Why would that be here? We knew Nancy wasn't murdered by anyone other than maybe accidentally Marilyn.

"Do you know if Samuel was wearing cufflinks?" I asked Thomas. Shuffling behind the wall, though he didn't look inside. I walked out the kitchen. He was sort of squatting against the wall, eyes closed.
"Likely, yes," he said. "Does it say his name?"

92

"Two S's," I replied. He opened his eyes.

"Next to the toilet? Why would he have lost one there? Was he wanking himself?" I laughed and then stopped because the picture of it came to my mind.

"I can't think of anything, it's a weird place to lose it," I said. Thomas thought for a second.

"Maybe he was getting himself a drink and lost it." How the hell would he lose one with that, though? I looked back into the kitchen. Countertop full of rings from the bottoms of the glasses.

"Unless it didn't have anything to do with what happened here, but with your uncle," I said. "He could've poisoned him here, before he even went outside with him."

Chapter seven

"His drink, you mean?"

"Yeah, his drink."

"So that would mean Walt was poisoned too," he said. His face shifted.

"Yeah, but not with the same poison."

"Maybe it was his cigar," Thomas suggested. "He could've done something to his cigar. His cigars were here too."

"I don't think so."

"Well, do you want to go find him? We can ask if it's his before making any connections."

"We should, yeah." He just seemed happy to be able to get the fuck away from the kitchen.

"Do any of you know where Samuel is?" I asked, walking into the sitting area with Thomas.

"Samuel? What do you need Samuel for?" Marilyn asked.

"You got me, don't you?"

Thomas didn't say anything but I could feel his annoyance. I got it, she was pushing it.

"We just want to see if our theory could be right," I said.

"Your theory?" Scott asked. I showed him the cufflink.

"Ah, now that *is* interesting," he said. "Do go on."

"We found it in the kitchen, next to the kitchen top the drinks were made on."

"And you think he may have dropped it while poisoning the drink," Scott concluded.

"Right, so where is he?" I asked.

"Unfortunately I haven't seen him since Mrs. Jones' passing," Scott said. Marilyn interrupted.

"The old fool is probably drinking himself to death in my father's study," she said. "Remember he wanted to get something different than a cocktail?"

"You're probably right, I don't think he knows about the wine cellar," Joan said. Hold on.

"*Wine cellar?*" I said. They both nodded. Since when was there a fucking wine cellar? Didn't I design the house?

"Do you want me to come along?" Jack asked. "I could do with some scotch."

"Yeah, we promised you one anyway, would be good to have another man with us," Thomas said.

"If you feel it's the right way to go about it, you can. I'll investigate the kitchen for any more clues surrounding the drinks. Maybe I've missed something before," Scott said and walked into the kitchen.

"I'll investigate the whiskey cupboard," Jack said. "Don't worry, it's in good hands." Thomas grinned a half grin.

"I'm sure, you're an expert," Joan said, patting him on the back.

"Should we sneak up on him and scare him?" Jack asked. We walked down the hall with the paintings again. It hadn't gotten any better from the last time we were there, the monkey and demon-like figure still hanging on the wall with their freaky friends. Usually freaky is good. With these paintings? Bad.

"Scare him?" Thomas asked.

"He'll get a heart-attack," I said. "He's probably drunk of his ass again."

"It'll be a funny sight though, don't you think?" Jack said. "We can all use it. Especially Thomas."

"I don't know what fun means," Thomas replied semi-jokingly. "It has died along with my hopes and dreams." And Nancy.

"Come on, it'll be great," Jack said.

95

"You know what, why not," I said. "Why the hell not." Jack nodded and looked excited. He was a bit of a man-child, but I still liked him better than Jason.

We approached the big wooden door of Walter's office, which was creaked open just slightly. Jack put his finger to his lips and started almost sneaking towards the door. Thomas rolled his eyes and laughed softly. Jack had his hand on the door handle and waited until we were there too. He counted from three to one on his fingers while mouthing the numbers and then pushed the door open, screaming. I screamed too and even Thomas managed to get out a small roar. Our screams quickly turned into horrified ones.

In the middle of the office was Samuel, straight on his back, with glass shattered next to him. His eyes wide open, staring up to the ceiling.
"What the fuck!" I yelled. Jack ran towards the body, checking for pulse. He looked concentrated for a second, then his expression changed.
"He's gone," he said.
"How long has he *been* gone?" Thomas asked in a state I can only explain as pure existential dread.
"Bloody hell, I can't tell. All I know is that he's *dead*," Jack said.
"Another god damn fucking body," I said and kicked a chair. "Fuck!" I stumbled up to Samuel's body and closed his eyes.

The body was still warm, he hasn't been dead for a long time. I tried not to look at his eyes while I closed them, but couldn't help but get another pair of dead eyes branded into my brain. The third body, this one wasn't even there in my original story. Me being here killed Samuel. I killed Samuel.

"I don't think I can take many more of those," Thomas said with a choked up voice. Jack put his hand on Thomas' shoulder.

"I'm starting to get tired of them too," he said.

"What do we do now?" I asked. This would look suspicious as hell. Besides, we still didn't know anything more about the cufflink.

"We gotta take him outside," Thomas said. "Who knows how long he's been dead, we can't waste too much time, he'll start to rot."

"Right, but again no stabbing or any other sign of aggression, beside the glass on the ground," I said.

"He probably dropped it when he fell," Jack suggested. "Glass can easily be a whiskey bottle or glass."

"Or he's been smacked on the head with it," I said. Jack shook his head.

"He would have a wound on his head. He doesn't. Maybe he got a heart attack while drinking and dropped to the ground. Look, there's even some fluid on the ground." He pointed to a small puddle of some type of liquid, though it wasn't the color of whiskey. This looked more like white vodka, very see trough. Like water, almost.

"I doubt it's whiskey," I said. Jack moved closer and looked at it. He stretched his hand out toward it.

"Don't touch it, it could be poison," I said.

"But why would it be here? It's Stonier's office, right?" Jack asked. "He's the guy that died first."

"Do you think he poisoned himself?" I asked. It'd be a stupid fucking story if he did, but it wasn't impossible. Though I couldn't see a reason why. Jack grew even paler.

"He should've," he said. "But I don't think he did. He loved himself too much for that."

"You got a point there," I said.

"Maybe the killer dropped it off in here after poisoning him. They probably didn't know the two of you and Samuel would go and drink bloody whiskey in here."

"Right, but no one looked scared that we would find out when we left just now, and I doubt it's any of us since we're all here. Unless that's the point, to make himself look innocent," I said and raised my eyebrows. "I'm getting a fucking migraine from all of the thinking." Jack and Thomas hummed in agreement.

"Is that a label?" Jack asked suddenly. He was squinting at the shattered glass.

"What does it say?" Thomas asked.

"I can't quite tell, it's kind of vague. I'm seeing something along the lines of Alohite," he said.

Alohite? He probably read it wrong, I didn't know anything called Alohite. Then again, I didn't know about the what-are-they-called pills Nancy had, so I'm not the best person to get for an investigation. I kneeled down next to Jack and tried to read the label. It did look like alohite, but the l could very well be a C, and the h maybe an N, that'd make more sense.

"Aconite!" I said. That one I did know, I researched it years ago for another book.

"Someone's excited," Jack said. "What's aconite?"

"A poison that's capable of instant death when ingested in large doses. Which, if the flask was even nearly empty at first, he did. And we can see it was pretty full, there's a fuck ton more liquid on the ground."

"He might've mistaken it for a shot of strong alcohol then," Thomas said.

"Exactly," I said. "It even has a strong burning, bitter taste, like let's say vodka."

Aconite, who would've thought? I couldn't help but let out a small smile, even though I genuinely was sad about Samuel's death. Just glad I was still good for something.

"Maybe it was used to kill Stonier too," Jack said.
"Yeah, maybe," I said. I squinted at the label again. Aconite. Huh. Something else was written underneath it, but just as the word above it, it was hard to make out. Even harder, this word was smaller.
"Hey, what does that say?" I asked.
"Hm?" Jack asked. I pointed, he squinted.
"Oh, Ginedair," he said. My hairs stood up. "That's that weird place." Ginedair. That name sounded familiar. Where did I hear that?
"What are you frowning about?" Jack asked.
"I could've sworn I saw it somewhere," I said. "This night." Ginedair. Right, it made me want to get gin. The little sticker on the bottom of Joan's shoe. Why would it be there?
"We really do need to get him downstairs, though. It's odd, it looks like he's just sleeping," Jack said. I straightened out my face.
"Yes," I said.

Stumbling through the hall we tried to carry Samuel downstairs. Past the big pots with roses once again, this time none of us drunk off our asses, nor had any of us just been naked.
"Careful!" Jack said to me. I nearly made a tumble down the many steps of the grand staircase. Another death was the last thing I wanted, especially my own.
"Right," I said.
"Don't let go," Jack said while we walked down the stairs. "If he falls, we all fall."

"Don't worry, I will never let go let go if you don't, Jack," Thomas said.

We stumbled down the stairs like Thomas and I had done before, but this time with a dead body instead of alcohol in our system. Samuel probably had enough in his for all of us. Funnily enough we still hadn't had any whiskey with Jack. Samuel weighed us down a bit, both mentally and physically. I honestly didn't expect him to die at all in this story because he didn't in mine. I killed him. If I hadn't come here, he'd still be alive. He even was a great help to Scott later on, kind of like a Watson to Sherlock. Maybe that's why he didn't have a motive. He was the Watson. Samuel didn't like him in the beginning of both stories and then learned Scott and he worked well together and shifted his views about him. Now he would never go through that shit. That bit was one of my favorite ones of the original story.

Jack walked into the sitting area, leaving Thomas, me and Samuel in the hallway. I could hear everything Jack was saying.
"We've got something, but it's not something anyone will like," Jack started. "Scott, can you come out for a second?" I could hear the door to the kitchen open and Scott walking in with his soft steps.
"What did you find?" He asked. "Was it Samuel's?"
"We haven't figured that out yet."
"Is everything okay?" I heard Joan ask. Thomas and I exchanged a look. It wasn't.
"It's a bit of a situation," Jack said.
"Go on," Scott said.
"What, did you wank each other off?" Marilyn asked.
"For once, Marilyn, can you please shut the hell up?" Jack said and sighed. "Samuel's dead."

"What?"

"He's dead. Poisoned, probably."

"Where is he?" Scott asked. Silence. Then footsteps coming towards us. Scott walked out of the room towards Samuel and checked his pulse.

"You are right, he has passed away," he said.

"No shit, Sherlock," I said. He looked me dead in the eyes.

"Very clever," he said. Jack walked up to us, together with Marilyn and Joan. So much for not sowing panic. They both gasped.

"Were there any clues as to how he passed?" Scott asked as he examined Samuel.

"A bottle of aconite was shattered next to him. We think he may have mistaken it for a shot of alcohol," I said.

"Aconite? Are you certain?" Scott asked.

"There was a label on it," Jack said. "So yes." Scott nodded slowly. I couldn't make out what he was thinking.

"Aconite poisoning doesn't show any signs in autopsy, acute poisoning at least. It would make sense with both mister Stonier and mister Singretti. The killer may have dropped it off after the fact, or perhaps even before, to lead any suspicion away. The question is now, who have been at the spot you found him?"

"Stonier's office," Jack said. "Don't you think we should take Samuel outside first? It isn't a very pretty sight, another dead body laying around in the hall." Scott stared at him for a second, then nodded.

"You're right, I got caught up in the details. Of course we should take him outside. Does anyone volunteer to help me carry him?" Jack and I grabbed Samuel.

"Can you open the doors?" Jack asked. Again, Scott stared at him for a second. I think we surprised him.

"Surely, yes, I can do that," Scott said.

Three bodies laid on the stones outside. Stonier's body had started to grow some ice. It felt like more and more of a fever dream, there was much more to my story than I had initially thought. It apparently wasn't a bad story, I was just becoming a bad writer. Missed whole plots and character backgrounds.

"Three bodies, huh?" Jack said. "How many more are to come?"
"Hard to say, hopefully none," Scott said.
"They all are so at random," Jack pondered.
"And at the same time all of them were killed by poison," I added.
"Exactly what I was going to say," Jack said.
"However two seem like accidents," Scott said.
"Seem, yes. How do we know if they're not planned? Maybe Stonier was the accident. Marilyn doesn't care about Nancy and Singretti as much as her father."
"Implying that Marilyn did it, that is," Scott replied.
"Who else could've done it?" Jack asked.
"Anyone, just as either of you could've committed the murders. Your placements around all of them were very suspicious."
"Yet you're talking to us about it," I said. Scott smiled briefly.
"I do not suspect either of you, no. I'm solely pointing out that anyone *could* have done it."
"Who do you suspect, then? Are you allowed to say?" Jack said.
"That I cannot say. But believe me when I say I am doing everything in my power to stop the injustice." He gave us a last nod and walked back inside.

"At least we're still alive," Jack said and grinned sheepishly. He tried being brave but I could tell that guy

102

was balls-deep in fear. I still wasn't, for some reason. I probably should be, knowing there could be poison or whatever other fucking lethal shit in any drink. I just didn't feel like it was that dangerous for me. Maybe it was the dream-idea, you're not as scared in dreams as you would be in real life because you know it's not real. It was like my senses were there but it was just an elaborate dream. I didn't feel like I could actually die.

Jack however was shitting bricks. This was the real fucking deal for him, obviously. And he did have a reason, people he knew for a long time were dying like dominos, one fell and they all went down. He could pretty much be the next. He genuinely could be, that was the bad part. He didn't die in my version but neither did Samuel. And guess what, we were standing right beside his cold corpse. Next thing you know that might be Jack. Or anyone else. But not me, for some reason. I didn't think I would end up there. Besides, I still thought Thomas did it. Especially after the rape-story came to light. Scott probably thought the same, he said he didn't suspect Jack or me. To be fair, we were my two other suspects. Who knows what Leonardo did before I came in?

"How about we stay sober for the rest of the night, maybe we'll escape death," I said.

"Any other day I'd be opposed to it but I can't say I disagree with that idea. I don't want to be next."

"I'm sure you won't be," I said.

"And neither will you," he replied.

I bit my lip out of habit and looked at Samuel.

"Wish I could say the same about him, I started to like him." Jack nodded and folded his arms.

"He was like an uncle to me, my father and he were friends." It was silent for a second.

"I heard about your father, I'm really sorry," I said.

103

"I appreciate it," Jack just said.

"Now they're both dead," he went on. "All I have left is Joan and my mother."

"And me, for as long as I don't die."

"And you. I know we weren't exactly friendly in the beginning of the evening, I hope you know I regret it," he said.

I was silent for a second, I didn't really know what to say. Never in any version of this story would I think Jason — Jack, would apologize. To anyone, but especially to me. I smiled and nodded. It did feel good. To hear him say that, even though he wasn't Jason. He didn't even know he stole Jessica. Jack didn't, he never had my competition in the first place. That wasn't even the reason for his apology, but it still felt really good.

"I know, it's alright. I was a bit of an ass to you too. I think I had judged you too soon," I said. He waved it away.

"I know what people think about me, don't sweat it mate. It's all good." I sighed and rubbed my hands together against the cold.

"It's not what I think about you, you just look exactly like a guy who did me wrong. I know you're not him, but it makes it hard to look at you sometimes."

"What did he do?"

"He was the guy my former girl cheated on me with. Joan looks a bit like her, is what made it even worse."

"That's horrible mate, I'm sorry. He sounds like a wanker," Jack said. I laughed. I based Jack off of him, it was weird as hell to talk about him to him. And for him to take my side, even weirder.

"He is. Glad you're not, though."

"Indeed. He must be handsome though, if he looks like me." I grinned.

"Gorgeous, but he doesn't quite beat you." Jack grinned too, then shivered.

"You wanna head inside? Could chat here all day but we'd end up like them," he said and gestured towards the bodies.

"I can't argue with that. Let's see if any more people have mysteriously died from poisoning," I said.

The atmosphere in the sitting area was even worse than before. Everyone looked down, even Marilyn. I don't know, I didn't think she meant to hurt Nancy. She probably felt really guilty about it, considering she helped her in a way. Nancy did it herself but Marilyn made it possible. Maybe she just acted nonchalant to hide the guilt she felt. She was an actress, after all. Joan sat next to Thomas, head on his shoulder, looking at nothing in particular. Scott was nowhere to be found and Marilyn dangled an empty glass in her hand, staring into nothing just as Joan and Thomas did. I didn't blame them, it was pretty late in the evening and there was a whole lot of new trauma unlocked. Me and Jack plopped down on a couch.

"Where's Scott?" I asked.

"Out being a sleuth," Marilyn said. She didn't change her staring to look at us.

"In the office?" Jack asked. She hummed in agreement.

"Marilyn not making any smart remarks, that IS new," Jack said.

"I'm just tired, I'll be back with a great one soon, don't worry," she said.

"How is she?" Thomas asked out of the blue.

"Who, Marilyn?" I asked confused. Thomas shook his head and looked at me.

"Nancy," he said.

"Dead," Marilyn said.

"I haven't looked," I said, ignoring Marilyn. "But I'd say she's as she was before."

"Dead," Marilyn said again. She put down her glass and took a new one.

"Would you mind bloody stopping with that word?" Jack said. "We know they are, you don't have to make it any more clear." I nodded.

"It's a bit insensitive," I added. As if she snapped back from her tiredness, Marilyn looked at us.

"Sure thing, Romeo and Julius," she said, smiling. She drank her drink in one big sip and put it down.

"Who's up for a game?" She asked.

"A game? Weren't you tired?"

"Funny thing about tiredness is that it can come and go as it wants."

"What, are you on crack?" Thomas asked. "We've lost *three* people in one night. What game do you want to play? Hide and seek? Next thing you know, someone else dies. Great to find, I can tell you that."

"A game of questions and commands," she said. I laughed. "Truth or dare? You want to play fucking truth or dare?"

"That's a good name for it, good one, Nardo," she replied.

"Marilyn, truth. Did you kill Nancy?" Thomas asked, interrupting us. Marilyn's face didn't give anything away.

"I did not. I've been saying that," she said. "Jack, have you sucked off Leonardo yet?" We frowned at the same time. Jack?

"Not that I recall, why?" Jack said.

"The two of you have been together a lot the last few hours," she said.

"Because we were carrying dead people outside, you moron," he replied. "You really are an unpleasant woman, do you know that?"

106

"Might be, but seems like I've hit a sensitive spot," she said with a grin. She stood up and turned the volume of the music up.

"What are you doing?" Jack asked with a tired expression.

The music filled the room. Marilyn didn't answer. Instead, she started swaying to the music. Waving her hands in the air to the rhythm of the music, eyes closed. She seemed all over the place. I exchanged a look with Jack and walked up to Marilyn. I carefully stopped her from dancing. "Come," I said. I took her hand and led her away. She didn't keep me from taking her with me, she didn't even say anything.

"Are you okay?" I asked her. We sat down in the library, just a few feet from where I sat with Thomas. It seemed to become routine to talk to a Stonier in the library after a death.

"It's alright if you're not," I continued. She stared at me for a while.

"You have very beautiful eyes," she said. "I didn't see that before." I raised my eyebrows and smiled.

"Thank you, you do too," I said. She smiled. The instigating vibe seemed to have melted away. Her eyes darted from me to the library and back. Almost like she was trying to focus them.

"Marilyn, are you drunk?" She frowned and smiled.

"Of course not," she said. "Are you?"

"Not anymore, no. I was, but I sobered up." Pretty quickly, too. Probably 'book magic'.

"That's good. Then both of us aren't drunk," she smiled.

She leaned against me and let out a big sigh. Drunk of her ass. I could smell the alcohol from her breath. Her hair tickled my neck. She was only one or two inches shorter than I am, so her head could pretty much lean against mine.

"You're really muscular," she said. She felt my arm with her hand. "You would never be able to tell from the suit." She looked up at me and smiled. What kind of backwards compliment was that?
"Thanks?" I said. Her smile grew even bigger.
"Anytime Nar," she said. I laughed.
"Nar?" I asked.
"It's like Narrator," she said. "You're always there."

I leaned my head back against the couch. Was that why that was my name in the story? Because I was the narrator? Jesus Christ, that's stupid. And it took me until now to figure out? By hearing it from a drunk Marilyn? I bit my lip and looked into the dark of the library. Fuck, it did suit my earlier writing. My subconscious at it's finest.

"Right," I said. Marilyn still looked at me, now with a questioning look on her face.
"I know something's up with you, you can try to play it off with alcohol and games but it doesn't hide it. It's not a bad thing to show it," I said. She stared at me. "Your dad died. Then the person you've spend a lot of fucking time with and then a guy who you've known all your life."
"I know they're dead," she said. "I know they're not coming back. I know what *death* means." She looked at the ceiling, head still on my shoulder.
"It's not your fault," I said.
"What if it is?" She said. Was it? Her voice shook slightly. I looked at her and sighed.
"It isn't, you didn't give her the pills with the intention to kill her, right?" I said. She shook her head.

"No," she said. She rubbed her neck. I put my arm around her and wiped a small tear from her face.

"And that's what matters. That's all that matters." She held my arm with her hand and sniffed.

"It's so messed up!" She said. "They're all dead!"

"But we're still here. All the rest of us, Scott, you, Joan, Jack and me. You still got us," I said. Until the end of the book, at least.

"But what if you die too? Or me?" I thought for a bit but didn't know what to say.

"That'd be fucked up," I just said. A weak smile came over her face.

"You can say that again," she said.

hapter eight

"Do they hate me?" She asked.
"Hate you? Maybe Jack, but I think he
did before any of this went down. I
don't think the others hate you." A little
laugh escaped her.
"Jack hates my guts," she said. I laughed too. He hated her
as much as I hated Jason, if not more.
"He does. But I don't. I like your guts."
"You stopped liking them a little while ago, I saw it," she
said. I opened my mouth and closed it again.

Did I? She looked at me with her big eyes. I guess when I
thought she was capable of killing her dad and Nancy I
disliked her a little bit, but I didn't hate her. Could anyone
hate that face?

"I did, but I like them again. I know you didn't mean to
kill Nancy."
"I didn't. I wanted to help her, she was very upset, I didn't
want to see her upset." I nodded slowly. I bet she was, I'd
be upset too if I had the counts baby inside me.
"I don't know if I can tell you, but it wasn't Thomas' child,"
she said. Huh?
"You knew?" I asked, pretty shocked.
"I don't know whose it was, but she told me it wasn't, you
know…"
"Consensual?" I said.

She nodded. She rubbed her forehead and tried to hide
the tears that came out of her eyes. I stroked her hair. It
made way more sense now, why she helped her. One thing

I was glad about is that she didn't know who's it was. That'd be traumatic to say the least.

"Hey, it's okay."

"It's so horrible," she said in a choked up voice.

"Does Thomas know you knew about it?" I asked. She shook her head.

"She asked me not to tell him, she wanted to tell him herself. I don't even know if she did. Do you think we should tell him?"

"He knows, he told me about it," I said. She sat up and looked at me.

"Do you know who's it was?" She asked. I waited a second too long with shaking my head.

"You know! You know who did it!" she said.

"I don't," I said.

"Yes you do. You think you're slick, but I see right through you. Who did it? There's going to be another body tonight, and it'll be that bastard who did it," she said.

"I can't tell you. I genuinely wish I could, but I can't," I said.

"Please, give me this one. I don't want to be hated," she said.

"And killing a guy will help you achieve that?" I said with a laugh.

"Maybe not, but it'll give Nancy peace. And Thomas, maybe."

"Seriously, you do not want to know."

"I seriously do. I'll seriously send him to hell."

"No," I said. I stood up and walked out of the library.

"Tell me!" She exclaimed and ran after me. She pinned me to a wall and though I could break away if I wanted to, I didn't.

"Marilyn, I can't tell you," I said. She slapped my arm, though not as hard as Joan hit my face, and let go. I didn't move.

"I deserve to know," she said with a slight tremble in her voice.

"You deserve to keep your peace," I replied. I crouched down against the wall. She couched down too.

"Please, so I know I didn't mess up for nothing," she said.

I looked at her. She had a desperate look in her eyes. Was she acting? I didn't know. Didn't think so.

"Please," she repeated.

"The guy you're looking for is already dead." I said. Her face turned disgusted.

"Samuel? I can't believe I was upset about his death," she said. It wasn't him, though not as far as I knew. I didn't say anything. She got a bit of a frown on her face.

"It's not him, is it?" She asked.

I slightly opened my mouth as if to say something but closed it again. Nothing I'd say would be the right thing. Silence wouldn't be the right thing either, but what could I say? No?

Her face froze. She sat there, looking me dead in the eye, not moving. I shouldn't have told her about the dead thing. I didn't know what to say, neither did she. I took her face in my hands, then hugged her. Her arms barely touched me back. It was like hugging a fish, just two limbs barely grasping. When I let go, she looked at me again, frozen. A tear ran halfway down her face over her pale cheeks. Face cheeks, that is.

"Shit," She said softly. She bit her lip and wiped the tear away. "Shit!" She said louder. "No!"

"That's what I said," I said like an asshole.

"How could he?" Marilyn said. She stood up and walked away.

"Marilyn?" I said. I quickly stood up and ran after her.

She went into the kitchen, I could barely keep up. Even though she was walking — admittedly, very fast — and I was running. My cardio wasn't that good, I hated cardio. "Marilyn, hold on, what are you doing?" I said while trying to keep up. She pulled a knife out of a knife-block and went into the sitting area.

"Marilyn wait!" I said. What the fuck was she gonna do with that knife? I ran after her into the sitting room. Jack, Joan and Thomas looked up surprised. I pointed at Marilyn, who was surprisingly walking past them. The knife wasn't even hidden, nor did she stop to look at any of them.

"She's got a bloody knife!" Jack said. The scattered and got away from Marilyn. She kept walking, right past them. Jack looked at me, confused, after which he stood up and ran after both me and Marilyn. Out the door she went, up to the balcony. Before I even got on to the balcony I heard a loud scream — from Marilyn — and some sort of sound, like something was hitting something.

"Marilyn, what the fuck are you doing?" I asked. She didn't even look up, knifing her father in the chest. She pulled the knife out and landed it his head, screaming with such an anger it legitimately sent chills down my body. She pulled it out again and managed to strike once more in his chest before I got to her and pulled her off of her father. This time she did resist. There wasn't any blood flowing from the wounds she made in the count's body. He was pretty frozen up already. Besides, he'd been dead for hours. The blood was probably puddled up on the bottom of his body.

"He's already dead, Marilyn!" I said. Jack ran onto the balcony, followed by Joan and Thomas.
"What in the bloody hell are you doing?" Jack asked.
"Marilyn!" Joan exclaimed. Thomas stood at the opening of the door, eyes wide open, not knowing what to do. Marilyn managed to get loose and jumped onto her dead father. Even *if* he wasn't dead before yet, he for sure was now. Jack had already taken the knife but that didn't stop Marilyn. She punched her dad in the face with closed fists. I tried getting her off again, this time with help from jack who'd given Joan the knife.
"Bloody hell Marilyn, get off of him," Jack said.
"He'll pay!" She screamed, half crying, half angry. "That bastard! I hate him!"
"He did pay, with his life," Joan said. "Twice, now." I couldn't tell if she was upset or confused.
Jack and I held Marilyn back, who was still trying to fight a — now literal — ghost.
"Let me go!" She yelled.

We slowly but surely managed to get back inside. Joan closed the door. Thomas still just stood there. Marilyn stopped fighting and cried. Jack let go and I lifted her up. We went back into the sitting area, all with a bit of a fucking adrenaline rush. I put her down on the couch and went to sit next to her. The rest of the group sat down too.

"What in the bloody hell was that?" Jack asked.
"She found out," I said, mainly directed at Thomas. He raised his eyebrows and then nodded slowly.
"I'll be damned," he said. "She does care."
"About what?" Jack asked.

"About Nancy," Thomas said. He briefly put a hand on Marilyn's arm.

"Would anyone mind to fill us in?" Jack said. I shot a quick look at Thomas. I wasn't going to say a thing unless he wanted me to. I learned my lesson with Marilyn. I knew even then that I shouldn't have. Thomas hesitated for a second but then sighed.

"Well, there goes the discretion. The child was Stonier's. Marilyn didn't know, but now she does. Obviously," he loosely gestured to the balcony. Scott came jogging in.

"What happened?" He asked. All of us pointed at the balcony. He ran off.

"Hold on, Stonier and Nancy were a thing?" Jack asked. Thomas and I shook our heads. His and Joan's eyes widened, Joan put her hand in front of her mouth and gasped.

"He raped her?!" Jack asked louder.

"That he did," Thomas said. I could hear the pain in his voice.

"That bloody bastard. I'm very sorry, mate," he said.

"How could he?" Joan said, choked up like Marilyn was before. Jack put an arm around her. Scott jogged in.

"Who and why. Explanations, now," he said.

"Calm down mate, the man was dead already. It's not a new murder," Jack said.

"It is not, but it is serious nonetheless. It's distortion of evidence, and very tasteless."

"Marilyn stabbed him after finding out he raped Nancy," Jack said. Scott's expression softened.

"Oh, I see," he said, a bit taken aback. His gaze went to Marilyn, who was still crying beside me.

"I'll still need to make record of it, but I won't leave out the reasoning behind it," he said. He walked up to me and Marilyn and stroked her hair. His presence still almost gave me butterflies. It's probably a narcissist thing, to like your story-self. I based him off of me in a lot of ways, after all.

"And I'm terribly sorry, Thomas, that's awful news to hear," he said.

"Thank you," Thomas said. Can't be nice for him to keep hearing and talking about his dead wife having been raped.

"Have you found anything out about Samuel?" Joan asked.

"It was indeed Aconite, as you all have suggested. My guess is that he mistook it for alcohol and had a sizeable portion of it, so big that he nearly instantly passed away. If it panned out the way I assume it did, I can say it was a quick death, so there was no prolonged suffering."

"Right, but he did die alone." I said. I remember that was his biggest fear. Scott looked at me, probably wondering how I knew. He was the one who found out in his questionings, after all. I should stop blurting shit out, I was the reason Marilyn went full slasher on her dad.

"He did, indeed. Tragic, but fortunately not a slow death," Scott said. He looked around the group.

"The only mystery now is who killed Stonier, besides Marilyn the second time," Jack said.

"You'd almost forget, wouldn't you? With all the additional death, that is," I said.

"Figure out who killed Stonier and you figure out who indirectly killed Samuel," Jack said.

"Marilyn, can I speak with you?" Thomas asked out of the blue. Marilyn looked up, wiping her tear-stripes away.

"Are you sure?" She asked. He nodded.

"I think we've got some things to clear up," he said. Marilyn waited for a second but then nodded. They stood up and walked away. So that's how it felt when I took people to other rooms to talk to them.

116

"Do you have any clues to who killed Walter?" I asked Scott.

"I have multiple different and contradicting leads. Everyone present is a very possible option," he answered.

"Everyone *alive*, you mean," Jack said.

"When you strip the diplomacy away, indeed. Everyone still alive is a possible option."

I leaned back on the couch and stared at the ceiling. I didn't know what time it was exactly but I'd say it was at least one or two in the morning. Usually that was no problem, I sometimes stayed up until five or six, just drinking alcohol with my cat as only friend, but usually I didn't have as much activity both mentally and physically as I did right now. I was almost sober now, I could get used to this. Drinking a fuck ton of alcohol and being sober just an hour later. Would be horrible for my liver, though. The white ceiling was absolutely spotless.

I heard Jack, Joan and Scott talking but I didn't bother to try and hear what they were saying. The music Marilyn had turned up was still at the same volume. Music from this time wasn't that bad. I wouldn't voluntarily buy it, but it wasn't that bad at all. I closed my eyes and bobbed my head to the music. If I fell asleep, would I wake up in my own house? Maybe. I wouldn't see any of them anymore, the only way to talk to them would be through writing. I wouldn't find out who did 'it' either. I'd have to write it myself. That'd fucking suck. I opened my eyes. Still bobbing my head, though. Was that where the expression 'This song is a bob' came from?

"Nardo, did you hear what he said?" Jack asked. I looked at him with a half-asleep face. Jack grinned.

"Clearly not. Would you be so kind to tell him again, Scott?"

"I'm about to look over my notes in the room in which I previously questioned everybody to see if I missed anything, so I'll be gone for about half an hour to an hour or so. I want to ask you not to run off anywhere until I come back, the same applies for Marilyn and Thomas when they return. I'd greatly appreciate it if you would pass on that message to them," he said.

"Yeah, sure thing," I said. Scott nodded gratefully.

"I do want to speak with you after, mister Berratare," he said and walked towards the small room. He turned around one last time.

"And please, do try to not kill any more people," he said, after which he closed the door behind him.

"Ah, he *does* have humor," Jack said.

We were back to how we begun. Jack, Joan and I in the sitting area. No Nancy this time, to make sure I was okay — or to find the dead count. No Samuel, who was, for as far as I remember from my story, slapping the count's face in a panic to try and wake him up — even though he would never wake up. Marilyn was talking things over with Thomas instead of doing whatever the fuck she was doing with Scott in the bathroom of the hallway towards the balcony. Thomas was actually around this time. And I was once again sober.

"Either of you hungry?" Jack asked.

"I could go for some food, yeah," I said. I hadn't eaten in hours. I'd had drinks, plenty of them. But no food.

"I'm not that hungry," Joan replied. "But you boys go ahead. I believe Nancy had some things ready. God, it feels like she is still in the kitchen," she said.

"And like Samuel is just getting drunk upstairs, ready to come down," Jack said. "But to be fair I don't mind old Walt being gone. He was a bit of an annoying geezer."
"Jack!" Joan said. Jack raised his hands and then gave her a quick kiss on the cheek. Weirdly enough it stopped annoying me.
"Come," Jack said to me and he went into the kitchen. Joan handed me the knife Marilyn used to express her anger. Joan had put it on the table, but understandably it was better off not in sight. I took it and walked after Jack.
"This doesn't count as leaving the sitting area, right?" I asked jokingly.
"Well if it does, we gotta sneak. He's one room away," Jack replied.
"You two have fun sneaking around," Joan said.
"You know what I meant," Jack said, laughing. I laughed too. Couldn't help it. We pushed the doors open and closed them softly.

"Look at that," Jack said happily and walked towards the multiple layers of food that Nancy and probably some other maids had made. Even though it stood inside some sort of food-closet, it did look good. I hadn't had food like that in I don't know how long. Maybe ever, seeing as the Stoniers were loaded. Jack grabbed a plate of fish that was laid out like you see in those 'you wish you had our life' commercials and some toasted bread things, those small pieces of bread you put something on and then eat as a snack. I think I've had one of those when my grandma died at the funeral. Tasted like her, can't lie. A mouthful of dry crumbles. He put it down on a small table inside the food closet and put some of the fish — salmon, I think, it was pink and smelled like one of my exes — on the toast. He proceeded to kindly hand it to me.

"How generous," I said and ate the thing in one bite. I despise people who say things like 'mouthgasm', but I had one. Fucking delicious.

"Wow," I said.

"Told you, mate," Jack said while chewing. "It's well worth it to be standing in a storage room for."

"Should we take one to Joan?" I said. Jack shook his head while loading up two more.

"She isn't hungry. Believe me, when she isn't hungry she will not eat."

"Right, she'll skip whole meals," I said grinning. Jessica did the same thing sometimes, she ate pretty well but if she didn't wanna, she didn't. One of our first dates I ended up eating for two because she wasn't hungry. Jack looked at me funny.

"My wife does the same," I said. No she didn't. I didn't have a wife.

"Ah, a women thing, maybe?" Jack said, and handed me another fish toast.

"Maybe," I said, though I was pretty sure it was just a Jess thing. Jack hummed in agreement.

"Well, I'm glad you've found someone you want to spend the rest of your life with," I said.

"Yes, I'm glad she's the one I picked out of all Stoniers."

"All? Aren't there only two?" I asked.

"Of course there's Thomas," Jack said. I laughed.

"Ah, right," I said.

"He's a better option than Marilyn," Jack said.

"Marilyn isn't that bad," I said. Jack rolled his eyes.

"You've known her for one evening, Nardo. Most of that time not even spent with her. Trust me, she's a nasty person."

"Things can change. I thought you were an ass at the beginning of the evening," I said. "And look at us now, eating fish together."

120

"Yes, but that was in the span of one evening. Marilyn has been a cunt for years. Doesn't change as easily."

"Thomas seems to have forgiven her," I said. He grinned a sour smile and wiped some crumbs from the table.

"Well, she didn't stab her father for me."

"That's fair."

"Besides, I didn't stab *her* either. Thomas did, with his bits." Right, a reminder Thomas fucked his cousin. Thank you.

"I heard," I said and coughed. I can't lie, I was a little uncomfortable. "He told me. You didn't, though?" I asked. I could've sworn by the way he hates her guts that they had a thing going for at least one time.

"Never. And I'm glad about it. She is a wench."

"Well," I said, but didn't finish.

"Brother, I know you've got the hots for her, but she's not worth it. Besides, she's with Scott," Jack said. "Are you a gentleman or the other man?"

"Is there really something to be the other man of?" I asked. "She met him just a couple of weeks ago, didn't she?"

"By a manner of speaking, you get what I mean, you knob." Oddly good morals for someone who was the other man in *my* life. He opened a box and looked inside. His face cleared up.

"Turkey wraps," he said and gave one to me. "Nancy made the best turkey wraps."

"I've never had 'em," I said.

"You will now." He took a bite and sighed. "Our people don't make them quite as good."

"No one is Nancy," I said.

"Truly. Her end was wholly undeserved. Especially the reason behind it," Jack said.

"Stonier was an awful fucking guy."

"He was, he was planning on taking Joan off his will too," Jack replied, mouthful of turkey wrap.

"He wanted to take her out of his will?" I asked.

"Only reason he couldn't yet was because the fellow who takes care of those type of things is out of town. He is supposed to come back in a week or so."

Was he now? Again, new shit popping up. What was it with this guy? Did he want to prevent Joan from getting money from the shares of jack's company after he died?

"Do you think that may have been the announcement he wanted to make?" I asked. Gathering everyone together to humiliate Joan. Cruel.

"I doubt it, he already told us. I don't know if he told the others but I don't think he'd do it through a celebration."

"Maybe he would, if Joan wasn't the only one getting striked from the will."

"Who else then? He won't strike Marilyn, she was his pride and joy."

"Thomas," I said. It made sense, the count didn't want to pay for his bakery. Thomas only had to wait. He'd eventually get the money after the count died. Jack looked at me and stopped chewing.

"Would he do that?" He asked.

"The man raped Nancy," I replied. Jack looked broody but didn't say anything. He swallowed the rest of the wrap he had still in his mouth but put down the left over part.

"Maybe, then. That's more motives. I don't think Joan did it, still."

She did get the whiskey he drank before he passed away. She could've put the poison in, knowing no one else but the count would drink that specific whiskey. No one else liked that whiskey besides him. Not the mention the sticker on her heel.

"Let's get back," Jack said. I nodded. He took out a sandwich, gave one to me and then left the storage closet. I hurried after him while taking a bite of the sandwich. Incredible, I should invest in better food when I got home. Dear god, it tasted good.

"Hey boys," Joan said when we came back into the sitting area. She was flipping through a magazine. I didn't know there were any, to be fair. I hadn't paid close attention to the rooms contents for most of the night. I was drunk for a big part and when that drunkness faded there was a murder every god fucking minute. It looked like a gossip-y type of magazine, not good content but good for taking your mind off of shit — something she could probably use right now. All of us could. Shit kept getting worse and worse.

"Hi darling," Jack said and tried to give Joan a kiss on her head. Joan ducked away without taking her eyes off the magazine.
"Don't kiss me with food in your mouth," she said, then looked up at Jack and instead gave *him* a kiss. "Mine isn't full of sandwich."
"Marilyn and Thomas not back yet?" I asked.
"No, they're really talking, I think. A good thing, hopefully."
"Yeah, hope so. We can use some reconciliation," Jack said.
"It's a nice change from the deaths," I added.
"I'm surprised we're still here," Jack said. "But I'm glad."
"Maybe this is a sign that better times are coming again," Joan said.
"Every second is a loaded gun until we can leave this god forsaken place," jack replied.

"Hm, maybe. Still, I don't mind the quiet." As if on cue, Marilyn and Thomas came back in.

"Hey guys," Thomas said. Marilyn was visibly a little happier than when she left. Tear stripes were dried up on her cheeks, but she was smiling again.

"Hey, how did it go?" Joan asked.

"Surprisingly well. Marilyn really had no clue about any of it, all she wanted was to help. I understand her," Thomas said.

"That's good to hear! Good of you two to talk it out," Joan said."We're okay again," Marilyn added. "At last."

"Hey, Nardo, can I talk to you for a second?" Thomas asked.

"You're on a roll, bud," Jack said. "Do you want to talk to me later too?"

"Just Leonardo," Thomas said with a laugh. His eyes stayed serious, his laugh only spread on the lower half of his face.

"Where do you wanna go?" I asked. What on earth did he want to talk to *me* about? We had a talk almost every hour so far. Honestly, the story derailed the moment I found the pills in Nancy's room, stopped actually knowing what was going to happen next right after her death.

"Dining room?"

"Yeah, sure. Lead the way."

The room was covered in a blanket of darkness, Thomas didn't seem to want to change it. The big, red, velvet curtains were put on the sides of the windows, showing the dark of the night. Stars lit up in the sky anywhere I looked. It was beautiful, I didn't remember the last time I saw stars. Thomas' face was lit up only by the light of the hallway. There wasn't a door, there were just pillars, holding up an archway toward the hall. There was however a door to the kitchen, but it was shut. Good

124

thing, probably. For Thomas. Good not to see it. Thomas sat down on the big, wooden dinner table and sighed. I could tell he was nervous, his hands were a little shaky, as was his voice.

"Before you say anything, this is me trying to make things right," he paused and looked at me. What did he do? I nodded and sat down next to him.
"Alright," I said.

I didn't know what he was gonna say. I hoped it was something positive, but he didn't seem too confident. He bit his lip and looked outside. I put my hand on his shoulder, other one on his chest, kind of trying to calm him down. Jesus fuck, his heart was beating fast.
"What's up?" I asked. With a moment of hesitation he sighed and looked me in the eyes.
"I helped kill Stonier."

Chapter nine

"*You* killed him?" I asked. I pulled my hand from his shoulder and chest. "Helped kill him, I didn't do the deed," Thomas replied.

"What's that supposed to mean?" I asked.

What the fuck. Thomas was one of the killers? Plural, apparently. He *was* my main suspect, but I didn't think he actually did it, for some reason. I don't think I really thought *anyone* killed him. And I in no way saw this shit coming. Him *admitting* it to me. He didn't say anything back.

"Who else killed him?" I asked.
"I can't say."
"So what was it? Was it the aconite?" Thomas looked me in the eyes and nodded. His eyes had a bit of a shine to them, as if he were about to cry.
"Did you kill Samuel too?" I asked.
"No, that's why I wanted to tell you. I don't want more people to die," he said. I looked away and sighed. What the fuck was I supposed to do with that. I didn't *really* blame him for killing Stonier, but it *was* the answer to the murder mystery. Halfway into the story at that.
"Jesus christ mate. What the fuck," I said. I still wasn't home though, probably because I didn't know the other killer. The one who, apparently, *really* killed him.
"How does telling me help?" I went on.

"Someone should know," he said. He genuinely looked upset. I stared him in the eyes, he looked away after two seconds.

"Mate, what are you playing at?" I asked. He looked back at me but didn't say anything. My heart sank through the floor. I knew that look. I'd *had* that look.

"No you're not. You're not fucking killing yourself."

"I can't go on," he replied, voice even less steady than before.

"Yes you fucking can. I'm gonna strap myself to you if that's what it fucking takes. You're not gonna drop that shit and disappear. Is this why you talked it out with Mari? You're on your good deeds before death shit?" Thomas looked away again and rubbed his eyes with his hand.

"I can't lose anyone else. Nancy is gone. Samuel is gone. My father's been dead for years, as is my mother. I helped *kill* someone. How am I supposed to stay?" He said. I was silent for a second, trying to find words. I understood what he felt, though our circumstances were different.

"The killing is a little unfortunate, but we're still here. You've got us, you've got Mari back in your life too. I don't blame you for killing him, if that helps." I put my arm around him, he put his head on my shoulder. He was a lot taller than me, so it was more a slumping than a resting pose.

"I understand you, but I can't let you go," I said.

"I know you can't," he said. "That's why I wasn't going to tell you."

"Asshole," I said softly. I slightly turned and grabbed his head between my hands, one hand on each cheek.

"You *will* be alright. Shit's gonna work itself out. I'll always be here. We're too far in now for you to give it up. We've survived for this long, I'm not letting you die tonight. We'll crawl if we need to, but we gotta keep going." A tear ran

127

down his face, I carefully wiped it away. I threw my arms around him, to my relief he hugged me back.

"It's hitting you, isn't it?" I asked. I felt him nod.

I wished I'd stuck to the story, in the original one he wasn't hit as hard. Nancy died in there too, but there he didn't wanna join her in the afterlife. He rubbed my back and let go. His eyes lingered for a second but then looked away.

"What are we supposed to do?" He asked.

"I don't know, I haven't been in a situation like this before," I said. "Do you know if the poison is anywhere else?"

"I didn't know there was any left, so I don't know," he replied.

"Alright, maybe Scott knows what to do," I said.

"Maybe."

"He went into his small 'office' some time ago, maybe he found something. Maybe he figured shit out."

"Or he found out I was involved," Thomas said.

"Did you cover your tracks?" I asked Thomas nodded.

"As good as I could, yeah."

"Well, maybe getting some sleep would do you good," I suggested.

"I don't think I can," he said.

"It's late, we've had a bad fucking night, even just resting with your eyes closed might help," I replied. "I get it if you can't tell me who did the deed. Just stay alive a little longer."

"I'm a moron," he said. "I should've never even thought about it."

"It's done now, you can't change it," I said.

I could, if I was still in my own house, being the writer. I would change it in a heartbeat. I'd write Nancy to stay

128

alive, too. And Samuel. Fuck, I'd write everyone except Walter to stay alive.

"Maybe I *should* try to get some sleep. Do you think Scott would mind?" He asked.
"I'm sure he won't, if he really needs you he'll probably get you." He nodded slowly and put his hand on my thigh.
"Thank you," he said. I rubbed his back.
"Don't mention it," I said.
"Think I'm gonna go upstairs for a minute, then. Really, thank you, Leonardo." I scoffed. Leonardo. I was lying as much as he was before. I was far from a businessman called Leonardo. I was no suit wearing smart guy. Thomas raised his eyebrows, questioning the scoff.
"Call me Mike," I said. He frowned.
"Mike?" He asked.
"Mike. I'm not Leonardo."
"Mike. Nice to meet you, Mike," Thomas said. He patted my knee and walked out the room, into the hall and up the stairs without asking any more.

I laid down on my back and stared at the upside-down window. The stars were no longer visible, dark clouds pulled up over the lands and toward the mansion. Thick flakes of snow landed on the windowsill and the grounds. More snow, just what we needed. I'd probably develop trauma's too, even though this world technically wasn't real. God, I was too sober for this shit. I knew me and Jack told each other to stay sober for the remainder of the night to escape death, but shit like this made it *really* hard. I just talked someone out of suicide, for now at least. I hoped he wouldn't kill himself after I went back to the real world. If I could get back at all. I fucked up the story so much I didn't even know a little bit where it could go next.

129

What if I died in this world? Would I really die or would I get back to the real world? Would I remember this story?

I traced the lines of the cold wood of the table with my fingers and sighed. I told Thomas my name. Could've been stupid. I doubt he would tell anyone, but I broke the fourth or whatever amount of walls there were in books. He probably thought I was a different person. I was, but I wasn't from his world. He probably thought I had some shady shit going on. Maybe I was. I don't know, maybe this *was* the real world. I could just as well be dead. I fell, hard. Maybe this was my purgatory. Figuring out who the fuck did it. I knew Thomas knew, that was something. He wouldn't tell me, but maybe later.

Who the fuck could it be? It legitimately could be *anyone*. Besides Samuel, maybe. Maybe even multiple people. Jack and Joan seemed up for it. Or Nancy, but in that case he would've told me, she was dead already. He didn't have to protect her. I slowly rose up and got off of the table. I really wanted to get a drink. I stared at the pillars underneath the archway. White marble.

I slowly started walking towards the hallway. Every step I made was loud. The click-clacking of my shoes annoyed the fuck out of me. Maybe I could find some shoes upstairs that I hated less. Not with Thomas, he was asleep, hopefully. Maybe the count's room, he was the only man still living here apart from some of the staff members. Living is a bit of an exaggeration, but you know what I mean.

Did he have normal shoes? Probably not, but anything was better than the shit I wore. I silently walked up the stairs, even though there was no need to be silent. It wasn't something I needed to do in secret, but I walked as silently as I could anyway. I passed the big pots of roses and the red drapes with golden ropes into the Stonier Family wing. I passed the paintings Joan collected and I passed Joan's old room where Thomas and I caught them naked. The carpet muffled the sound my shoes made enough to walk normally without wanting to cut them off of my feet.

"Nardo?" Echoed through the hall. A click-clacking of heels came up the stairs in a running pace. "Is that you?" Marilyn poked her head around the corner of the drapes and the pot. When she saw me, she started running towards me.

"Hey, where is Thomas?" She asked.

"He's gone to bed," I said.

"Is he okay?" She said with a concerned look. I pursed my lips for a second and nodded.

"Just tired," I lied. Half-lied, likely. I was tired too, I bet everyone was feeling it.

"Oh, alright," she said and paused. "What are you doing upstairs, then? Are you tired too?"

"No, I'm trying to find different shoes," I said. She frowned.

"They don't really fit me and I thought I'd be home by now," I explained. "I figured your dad would have some lying around I could use." The frown dissipated a little bit but didn't go away completely.

"Do you want me to come along?"

"Are you sure you want to go into your father's room after what happened?" I asked. She put up a half crooked grin.

"I'm not gonna burn the place down if that's what you mean," she said.

"Good. Fine, come along," I said.

The cold, white light of the moon shone into the room. Perfect timing, because after a few seconds it was back behind the clouds. All we were left with was the light of the hallway. This time I didn't bother to turn on the light. A big bed stood against the left wall, exactly in the centre as far as I could tell. Two massive wooden nightstands beside it and a wooden headboard behind it. A sitting area in the left corner closest to the door, with a small liquor cabinet beside it. A giant closet spanned over the entirety of the right wall, with a couch in front of it and a mirror next to the couch. I walked up to the shoe-part of the closet and tried squinting my eyes against the dark. I saw some navy colored loafers with white strings and took them out.

"What do you think?" I asked and showed them to Marilyn.
"They look comfortable," she said.
"But not good?" I asked.
"They're loafers, what do you want me to say?" She asked with a small laugh. She walked past me to the shoe rack and after a few seconds of scanning it, she pulled out black leather shoes with a slight pointed toe.
"And that is good?" I asked.
"Try them on," she said and handed them to me, then pointed at the couch. I sighed and sat down. I undid my old shoes and stepped into the other ones. They were comfortable as fuck. I wouldn't have guessed from the look of them. I looked up at Marilyn, who was rummaging through the closet.
"What are you doing?" I asked. "I've got them on." She pulled out a black suit jacket and pants and handed them to me.
"Mari — are you kidding me? There's no way I'll fit them," I said.

"Trust me," she replied. I rolled my eyes. She turned around and took out a black dress shirt.

"With this," she said. I looked her dead in the eyes.

"Go on, it's dark, don't worry about me looking," she said. I sighed, looked at the ceiling and took my jacket off, then handed it to her.

"I wasn't," I said. I started unbuttoning my shirt. At least she didn't pick more blue for me. Button by button I felt the cold come in. It wasn't that thick of a shirt, but it apparently kept out the cold pretty well.

"Fuck, it's cold," I mumbled.

"You want me to warm you up?" I heard Marilyn say. I paused and looked at her. I could feel my blood flow change.

"Don't do that," I said. She raised one eyebrow. Her dark hair gleamed in the soft light. I breathed out sharply and looked away for a second, then back at her.

"You're with Scott."

I unbuttoned the last button and handed her the shirt. She slowly stepped closer and touched my stomach. She traced the line in the middle of my abs, electric streaks shot down. Her hand lingered for a second. I took it and placed it on my chest. She laughed softly at the fast beat of my heart.

"Now you know what you do to me. Please, stop it," I said. "I'm really trying here." She pulled my hand to her lips and kissed it, then sat down on the couch. I rubbed my chin and inhaled deeply. I took the black shirt and put it on. Surprisingly, it fit my arms pretty much perfectly, unlike the blue shirt. I actually had shape in this one.

I took off my belt and pulled down my pants, facing away from Marilyn.

133

"I like your butt," she said. I laughed.

"And I like yours." I heard her standing up from the couch again. For fucks sake. I couldn't keep this up forever. Her hand traced my spine, down to my butt. I looked over my shoulder, right at her. She was smirking, as expected. She knew what the fuck she was doing. She walked over to face me, hand still on my body. She left it on my chest. Heart still beating like a motherfucker.

"Do you want me to put this suit on or not?" I asked. To be fair, I didn't want to anymore. She didn't say anything, but started slowly buttoning my shirt. The goddamn smirk still on her face. I couldn't do anything but look at her. Fuck, she was good. She buttoned the lowest button and brushed the lowest part of my stomach. More electricity shot down. She smiled and stepped away.

"I *do* want you to put it on," she said. "It's a good suit." I looked at her and scoffed. I pulled the other pants up. I should've put on my shoes after I changed pants, but I managed to get them on despite the shoes. Even though they were the count's pants, they fit really well.

"All you need is a belt," Marilyn said and searched in a drawer. She pulled out what looked like a black leather belt, though with snake print and a gold buckle. She made me look like a fucking mob boss. She smirked and slowly put the end through the loops of my pants. She stepped closer to get it through the holes on the back and very obviously touched my ass.

"Mari," I said. She laughed and pulled the belt through the remaining loops. She closed the buckle and swiftly brushed against my dick. I rubbed my face with both my hands and looked at her.

"It looks good on you," she said. I looked her in the eyes, she looked back with a grin. I shook my head and laughed.

134

"Fuck you," I said and put the jacket on.

Fit just as well as the other parts of the suit. You could see my muscles in this one, contradictory to the blue suit. Who was in charge of costumes in this story anyway? The blue one didn't suit me for shit. I reached for the tie on the couch but she stopped me.

"You look better without it," she said, then unbuttoned the two highest buttons. Not as slowly as before, she seemed to genuinely try to make it look good this time.
"What, the tie or the suit?" I asked. She smirked but didn't reply. She looked at me for a second, went with her hand through my hair to style it and smiled.
"Your hair is really soft," she said. I let my hand glide through hers.
"So is yours. Wow, your hair is nice." I brushed through it again. She stopped me from doing it a third time and took my hand.
"Are you up for a drink?" She asked, glancing in the direction of the liquor cabinet. Was I? I wanted to, if only to forget about the shit going on outside the room. Besides, Jack was probably drinking again too. Who wouldn't? I nodded. She grinned and pulled me towards the cabinet.

Flasks upon flasks of equally good looking liquor filled the shelfs, like they did in the office, just in less big amounts of bottles. Some brandy, a few insanely old wines and whiskey. A shame the count wouldn't be able to drink them anymore. That bastard didn't deserve them. We did, though.
"What do you want?" Marilyn asked.
"Maybe no whiskey, I don't wanna take the chance," I said. She frowned.

135

"Poison," I said. "You never know."

"Fair enough," she replied. "Brandy?"

"Yeah, why not?" I said and took out a bottle of which I couldn't read anything on the label besides the big letters 'BRANDY'. I poured two glasses and unlike with Thomas we drank it in parts. Still, we finished one after another quicker than most.

Every sip I felt the thoughts glide away. I knew it would just delay them, but I didn't care. It was what I did, I delayed. Usually in worse company than I was now, Marilyn looked even better with every glass I drank. Her dark blue eyes became more seductive than they already were before. We both got drunker and drunker, I couldn't tell how many glasses we already drank but I knew it felt like the good thing to do. Maybe not the better thing, but good nonetheless. Really good. I shouldn't have stopped drinking to begin with.

We sank down onto the huge bed. I hazily looked at the ceiling, it had paintings on it like that one famous church. Not as weird as the ones Joan brought home, these were biblical for as far as I could tell. Angels and shit like that. I rolled over to face Marilyn who was looking at the ceiling too. She turned her head and smiled a smile with teeth and all.

"I like you," she said. I laughed.

"You don't say," I said.

"I do, I enjoy your company."

"That's good to hear," I said with a stupid little smile on my face. I carefully brushed through her hair. How did she get it that soft?

"If you didn't have a thing with Scott I would," I said.

"I know you would, baby," she said. "Me too." She turned her head to face me, I looked down at her. I wasn't a flattering sight, but she was.

"I appreciate your respect, Nardo," she said.

"Ofcourse," I replied. "But I'm here if shit goes south. Just call and I'll come running." She laughed and looked back up at the ceiling.

"I'm glad you were here today," she said. "Even though it would've been better for you to not be."

She could say that again. I made a huge mess of the story. I did know who partly killed Stonier and what killed Nancy, but I came across things I didn't need to know and did things I shouldn't have done too. Hook up with Marilyn was one, but it was one I didn't regret as much as the others.

"Me too," I said. "It's worth the shit."

"More or less," she said. She sat up and looked out of the window.

"I want wine," she said and walked over to the liquor cabinet. Wasn't a very steady walk.

"You sure? We've had a lot," I replied.

"I'm sure." She took out a round, green bottle and held it up triumphantly.

"You want some too?" She asked. I sat up on the bed and leaned back on it with my hands.

"Yeah, I guess."

With a loud pop she uncorked the bottle and shakingly — thanks to the big amount of wine inside, she couldn't hold it still because it was going back and forth inside the bottle — poured some in a glass. She took out another glass and just as shakingly brought the bottle to it, though

137

this time some of it missed the glass and dripped onto the bottom of her dress.

"No! My dress! I'm never going to get that out!" With a big, annoyed sigh she put the wine bottle back onto the shelf and tried rubbing the stain. Obviously that made it worse.
"Damnit!" She said.
"It's fine, don't worry. You barely even see it from this distance," I lied.
"Really?"
"No," I laughed.
"God, I have to change. Come," she said and walked out the door.

We strolled through the hallway towards Marilyn's room, holding onto each other for balance. I wasn't as drunk as before but it passed the point of being able to walk normally. We passed some more weird paintings but I barely even looked at them anymore. Exposure therapy, the longer you face shit the more used you get to it. She opened a big wooden door and went inside. It wasn't as big as Stonier's door, but it was still a big fucking door. She gestured for me to come in and flicked the light on.

Her room was very big, her bed coming close to the size of Stonier's. She had dark red silk sheets. Ofcourse she did. A chandelier hung from the ceiling, the light reflecting from the thousands of crystals — or diamonds, I couldn't tell. A big, black rug laid underneath and around her bed. The floor was dark wood, polished so hard it shined. She had a small sitting area too and her closet was even bigger, it was a walk in closet the same width as Stonier's but a lot deeper. Rows upon rows of clothes and jewellery hid behind the glass doors.

"What color should I do?" She asked.

"Match me. Do black," I said. She smirked and opened the glass door to her closet. With a concentrated look she rummaged trough her own closet as she did with her father's to look for a suit for me. She was beautiful. With a content look she pulled out a black velvet dress.

"What do you think?" She asked.

"I like it, put it on," I said. Without skipping a beat she turned around and reached for the zipper, but seemed to struggle.

"Need some help?" I asked. I knew she damn well could reach it. It was Marilyn. She looked back over her shoulder and nodded.

With a sweep she cleared her hair from her back, swinging it over her shoulder. I grabbed the small open circle on the end of the zipper with my thumb and pointer finger and slowly pulled it down. With my other hand I kept the top pieces of the dress in place while I zipped it down. The red silk of the dress felt smooth, it matched her bedsheets. I moved my hand across her shoulder and with a smooth move shoved her dress strap from it. She turned around to face me and with a smirk she shoved the other off of her shoulder. The dress almost flew down, she grabbed the top of it and held it close in front of her.

"You sure you don't want to?" No, I did.

"Yeah," I replied with a pained face. She rolled her eyes and raised her eyebrows.

"Was worth a try," she said and turned back around.

I walked up to the bed to keep myself from changing my mind and sat down. She let go of the dress and stepped out of it. She wore one of those old timey underpants, but for whatever reason it still looked good as hell on her. It wasn't the *best* look, but she could look good in anything.

It was sort of high wasted, reminded me a little of grandmas. She *would* be in my time if the timeline was accurate, was a bit of a weird thought.

"I like your butt," I said. She looked back and smiled. "And I like yours." She stepped into the black dress, this one didn't have a zipper. It looked more stretchy, more than the other one. She grabbed the red dress, threw it to me, walked toward the bed and lied down next to me. I tied the dress around my neck like a scarf and lied down beside her. She rolled over and put her head on my stomach. We laid there for a few minutes, both looking at the ceiling.

"How would you kill someone?" Marilyn asked after a couple minutes.
"Kill someone?"
"Would you use poison?"
"In an ideal killing? No. I'd strangle them. Poison is good in stories but in real life I wouldn't use it to kill someone."
She nodded slowly.
"A crime of passion," she said. I laughed. Sure.
"What about you?" I asked.
"A shot," she said. "Quick and clean."
"That is only if you shoot right the first time, I would fuck up and shoot them in their arm."
"My aim is good," she said. I sat up on my elbows and looked at her. Her head fell down to my lap. She moved her head a couple times and smiled. She felt it.
"How good?" I asked.
"Very good," she replied. "I'm a good shooter."
"Really?" I asked with a slight disbelief in my voice. She nodded and smiled.
"Show me." She frowned surprised and looked at me.
"Now?" She asked. I nodded.

"Now." She stared at me and a smirk came onto her face. She sat up and scooted closer.

Before I could protest she wrapped her arms around my neck and kissed me. I grinned and went along. She might've been fictional but she had her kissing down. I could taste the fruity brandy we drank just minutes ago. I put my hand on the back of her neck and pulled her down on the bed again. I wish I could take her with me after the book was finished. Why couldn't I have a Marilyn in my world? The real world, I mean. After who knows how long she pulled back and winked. I felt a little bad but I was too boozed up to care about Scott's feelings. I grimaced. I was the Jason in this story.

"Let's shoot some shit," Marilyn said.

Chapter ten

She walked over to her makeup table and opened a drawer. With a quick move she pulled a gun out of a hairbrush — don't fight me on this, it was a very big hairbrush, the part with the trigger was inside the part with the prickly things you brush your hair with and the long thing that shoots the bullet was inside the handle — and held it up with a smile. It was a steel with wood small handgun with a long, what do you call it? The part that was hidden the the handle.

"Oh, that's sick, I thought you were talking about—," I said, laughing.
"No, I meant actually shooting." She did a quick bow and walked back over to me.
"What do you want me to shoot?" She asked with a crooked grin that told me she too felt the alcohol. Was it a good idea? If she could shoot straight when sober she probably had less good of an aim now after she drank a fuck ton of alcohol.
"Let's shoot something that doesn't feel pain," I said. "A plant or some shit like that." She laughed and loaded the gun with a bullet.

I peeped my head around the corner of the door and looked around the hallway. More paintings, naturally. Wouldn't be that fun to see get shot. At the end of it I saw a black-and-white vase, stood on top of some kind of high dresser. I pulled Marilyn closer and pointed.

"The vase," I said.

"Yes sir," she said.

She dramatically stepped into the hallway, went to stand sideways and closed one eye. She seemed to focus for a few seconds — maybe to focus her gaze from the alcohol, maybe genuinely to determine the best place to shoot the thing. Her finger pulled the trigger and the bullet shot out of the gun. It shot through the air, pushing it away with it's rounded point. A figure walked around the corner of the hallway and past the vase. The bullet ripped through the the figure, leaving a path of blood and what the fuck more came along on the wall and floor and the bullet flew through the vase. Thomas' head jerked while the blood squirted out to the beat of his heart and he fell to the ground, into his own blood. A wave of panic flooded my body through my stomach into my chest.

"Thomas!" I yelled and ran toward him. Marilyn screamed. I kneeled down by Thomas, Marilyn following shortly after. The fear built up inside me, a hole sat right in his neck.

"Thomas," I said. He looked up at me with fear in his eyes, then went limp. I bit my lip and tried to control my upcoming emotion. Marilyn let out a cry and fell down on her knees next to us. I couldn't pull my eyes away from his head. Blood started flooding the floor while his beautiful eyes stared me down like his wife's did. This time was different, I actually got to know Thomas. Motherfucker, got killed half an hour to an hour after I told him to stay the fuck alive. I grasped his head in a wild flow of terror and sadness. I felt his warm blood run over my hands onto the ground. I tried and failed to stop the blood by putting my hand on the wound.

"Thomas, wake up," I said with a barely there voice. The lump in my throat kept the sound from coming out almost entirely. I could barely see through the fucking tears that came into my eyes. I tried yelling but it barely came out, swallowed by the tears. I put his head against mine.

"Don't go," I said. I barely noticed Marilyn's cries, my head was filled with white noise.

"We have to hide him," Marilyn managed to get out.

"Before they see." I shook my head and tried swallowing my tears.

"I can't. I can't leave him."

"We have to, come," she said and tried pulling him up while the tears streamed down her face. "We have to, please!"

"No!" I yell-cried. She ripped a piece off of her dress, shoved my hand away from his neck and wound the piece of dress around his neck to stop the bleeding as good as she could.

"Hello?" Jack's voice said from the bottom of the stairs, at least 50 feet away. Marilyn and I looked at each other in pure terror and tried being as silent as possible. Marilyn tried lifting Thomas again, but didn't get much farther than an arm.

"Nardo, please," she whispered desperately.

I pulled Thomas from the ground onto my shoulder and tried standing up. My legs could barely hold me up, let alone me and Thomas. Marilyn tried supporting the weight as good as she could. As silently as we could we walked the opposite way of where Jack was.

"Who's there? Everything okay?" We heard. I could barely see, stumbling along the walls of the house we moved forward, step by step. I couldn't feel anything, it felt like the walls were turning and the house was spinning on it's own axis. The floor was wax and it wanted to eat me

144

whole. Thomas was dead. I killed him. I killed him and Samuel. Marilyn's hand led us through the house. I *killed* Thomas. Every step I took I felt his head bonk softly on my back.

"Hello?" Jack's voice echoed in my head and through the halls. Then a loud yell.

"Oh my god," the walls said. Oh my god, my head said. I stopped and tried to find balance against the wall, Marilyn pulled me along and further away from Jack. My eyelids wouldn't close, I could do nothing but look. Look at what I did, his legs on my chest and his feet by my thighs. Tears ran down my cheeks. I let out a soft, desperate cry. I could hear Joan's heels click up the stairs in the distance, searching for her husband.

"Jack?" She yelled. Marilyn pushed us through a door and softly closed it. Her breath quickened and she let herself glide onto the floor.

"Oh my god," she whispered and put her face in her hands. I put Thomas down as carefully as I could. We heard a second scream as Joan discovered the pool of blood and shattered vase.

"We have to go on," Marilyn said with a choked up voice.

"To where?" I asked with a monotone one. I couldn't think. My head was empty.

"The covered balcony on the side," she said. "No one will come."

I nodded but I didn't know if I actually was so I nodded harder.

"Okay." I picked Thomas up and hung him over my shoulder.

We walked down the stairs to the hallway that led to the balcony with the count, Nancy and Samuel on it. There was a big room on the bottom of them with a couple of doors, one of which I knew was the way to said hallway with the big balcony. We went through the door and immediately through another door on the left. The cold of outside barely touched me, all I felt was my tears blow away by the wind. I gently put him down on the ground and fell down next to him. I wrapped my arm around him and closed my eyes. The tears wouldn't come out but my lip was stuck quivering.

"We have to get back inside," Marilyn said while she tried to help me stand up.
"I can't leave him here," I managed to get out. "No one knows where he is."
"If we stay here, they will," Marilyn said. Her tugs grew more desperate the colder it got.
"Nardo!" She said.
"They'll know," I said.
"They won't, keep your voice in control," she said. I finally gave in to her tugs. With a relieved sigh she hugged me. I threw a look at Thomas and tried not to let the emotion get through.

Marilyn was right. We had to get back before anyone noticed us missing, along with Thomas. Marilyn pulled me through the door and closed it, separating me and Thomas. Feeling slowly came back to my hands as I moved them. Surprisingly enough, we barely got any blood on us. A lot on my hands from when I held his head but our clothes were fine, except for the piece of fabric Marilyn ripped off of it to bind Thomas' neck.

"Oh, the piece of dress," I mumbled. "They'll know."
"Oh, I forgot!" Marilyn said and she slipped through the door only to come out some time later with the piece of fabric, drenched in blood. She walked to a bathroom and

146

threw it in the trashcan. She wasn't good at covering up tracks. I didn't care. I washed my hands in the sink. The water felt warm, but it was set on cold. My hands were colder than the water. I stared down the sink as the blood flushed away. Marilyn's hand ran up and down my back in a very different way than it had just a while ago.

"Do you want to put your other dress back on?" I asked. "The one you're wearing is missing a piece."
"You're right," she said. I untied the dress I still had around my neck and handed it to her. She slipped in and out of the dresses before I could bat an eye, stuffing the black dress on top of the bloody piece of fabric in the trash. Still not very good at covering her tracks.
"Come," she said. We walked through the hallway that led to both balconies and back into the sitting room. We didn't wait too long and walked to the staircase in the main hall.

"Jack? Joan? Is everything okay?" Marilyn yelled. They came running down the stairs, faces pale white. I sniffed, stood upright and tried to look as normal as possible. I tried getting Thomas' eyes out of my head, but they stared at me through the walls.
"There's blood everywhere!" Jack yelled.
"What? Where?" Marilyn asked.
"Upstairs, there's a pool of it."
"Where's Scott?" Joan asked.
"I don't know, I haven't seen him in a while." I said with a numb mouth.
"Do you think it could be his?" Marilyn asked.
"It can't be, right?" Jack asked, looking at Joan.
"I don't know!"
"Where's Thomas?" Jack asked.
"He went to bed, he wasn't doing well, everything that happened to Nancy hit him all of a sudden," I said.

"Poor man," Joan said. Jack walked up to the door with blinds in front of it and pulled it open. Scott was inside, he looked up a little startled but quickly composed himself.
"Oh god," Joan stammered. "So it's Thom."
"What is the matter?" Scott asked and stepped out of the room.
"There's blood everywhere," Joan said.
"Upstairs," Jack added. Scott didn't hesitate a moment and sprinted through the room and up the stairs.
"Where?" He yelled while running. Jack ran after him.
"In the east wing," he yelled.
"I hope Thomas is okay," Joan said and hurried upstairs.
Marilyn and I looked at each other, completely mortified, then ran along with the others.

The soft carpet was still wet from the blood, the blood on the walls was dripping down and made long paths of red. "Fuck," I said. I tried my best not to see Thomas lying in the puddle, neck blown to bits. The part he fell on was still slightly less soaked than the part he bled on directly. If you looked carefully you could even see his shape. Why couldn't I have written a parody of a comedy or romance novel? This wasn't even that exaggerated, it was just like a normal detective novel. Scott looked around the group.

"Where is Thomas?" He asked.
"He told me he was going to sleep," I said. I felt numb. This must be what Thomas was talking about in the library. I didn't hear my thoughts. I didn't know if I even had thoughts. Scott rushed away to the west side of the building where the staff's rooms were.
"Do not touch *anything*," he said. The carpet pulled my eyes in and didn't let them leave. It wasn't just blood. There was other shit too, some on the walls, some had dripped down. I looked away and turned around. All I saw

was Thomas. In the blood, in my head. Dead Thomas, bleeding Thomas.

"Are you drunk?" I heard Jack say.
"Drunk?" I asked.
"Drunk," he said. I shook my head. He grabbed my shoulder and looked me in the eyes.
"Yes you are, stupid. I thought we were staying sober," he said.
"I couldn't," I said, trying not to get choked up. He frowned concerned but hugged me.
"Hey, man, I get it, it's rough," he said.
"I hope Thomas is okay," I said with a quivering lip, though luckily no one saw because Jack was still hugging me.
"It can't be anyone else," Joan said. "We're all here, except for Tho-," Marilyn shushed her. I gripped Jack closer, he rubbed my back. His hands were warm, I'd warmed up again but they were still warmer than me.
"It'll be okay," he said. "You're okay." If only Jason was like Jack.

Scott came running back in, unreadable as ever though his voice told me he was genuinely worried.
"He is not asleep in his room," he said. I let go of Jack and we both faced Scott.
"Where else *could* he be?" Jack asked. Joan pointed at the blood-red carpet stain.
"Where is his body? You'd think there would be a body, right?" Jack asked.
"Unless someone deliberately hid it," Scott said. "Who found the blood?"
"We did," Jack said. "Joan and I found it."
"Was there any sign of Thomas?"
"No, just blood."

149

"It must be from a gun," Joan said.

"How can you tell?" Scott asked.

"You disagree?"

"Not quite. I'm only asking how you can tell."

"The splatter on the wall along with the broken vase. It must be a gun."

"But I didn't hear one," Marilyn said,

"We did, it's why I went upstairs," Jack said.

"We need more gun control," Joan said.

"We have enough gun control, what we need is idiot control," Jack replied.

"Would all of you please get to the sitting area?" Scott asked. We nodded in unison.

"Except for mister Berratare," Scott added.

I stopped moving and looked at Scott from the side of my eye. Why me? I shot a quick look at Marilyn, but she didn't look back at me. Smart move, to be fair. I looked suspicious as a motherfucker.

"Alright," I said. The three others quietly left the hallway, after a few seconds I heard their heels and Jack's shoes going down the stairs. I could feel my heart beat in my chest but I tried to keep a pokerface. Did he know? He was a detective, he probably did. Fuck. I turned to Scott, to the left of the pool of Thomas' blood.

"I trust your judgement," Scott started. "You've been very accurate in some matters, something I can only mark as impressive." My judgement? I didn't say anything, I didn't know what he knew or what he didn't. Maybe this was a technique to get me to speak up about Thomas, not talking would do me better than talking. Scott smiled briefly.

"I could use some help in the case," he said. "If you're up for it." I frowned in surprise and looked at Scott. Help in

150

the case? Why would he want *me* to help? Scott's face stood genuine for as far as I could tell. He needed my help? Was this the part of the story where Samuel helped him out before? Samuel wasn't around anymore, maybe I was the next best thing.

"My help?" I asked.

"Yes. I would appreciate it. We have been on the same page on a great many occasions. I believe a fresh set of eyes could help this investigation. Your eyes, to be precise." Because I knew what was going on, in the first half at least. I didn't anymore. It did however give me the opportunity to lead him away from me and Marilyn's trail.

"How can I help?" Scott kneeled down by the pool of blood and gestured to it.

"What is your first thought?" He asked.

"It's an awful lot of blood," I said. He nodded.

"A lot of blood means a lot of blood loss. It must've pierced a vital body part or artery, maybe multiple. Joan was right about it being caused by a gun."

"By a gun? I don't think anyone here has one," I said. I didn't think anyone knew about Marilyn's gun, she'd be safe.

"If we can pinpoint who has access to a gun, we'll know who did it."

"Don't you have a gun?" I asked.

"I don't have it on me today. I did not expect to be investigating when the day started," he replied. Right, he came for a party.

He stepped over the blood to the dresser. He looked around for a bit, then picked up a small, kind of oval thing from behind some shards of the vase. He held it up to the light and cleaned the blood off of it. The bullet. In a flash I saw it hit Thomas' neck. I sniffed and blinked. Shouldn't have had the alcohol. This wouldn't have happened, first of all. Secondly, I wouldn't look as nervous.

"We'll have to find the gun that fits with this bullet," Scott said, studying the bullet's bottom. "A point thirty two bullet, S&W. Smith and Wesson." I had no fucking clue what any of it meant. I never researched guns, just poisons.
"Does that tell us anything?" I asked.
"It does, it is most likely a civilian handgun. These guns usually have a wooden grip, it's what sets them apart. Find the gun, find the culprit." Fuck, hopefully Marilyn hid the gun somewhere no one could find it, unlike we did with Thomas.
"So where do we look?" I asked.
"It could be anywhere. Most likely hidden. We do need to find Thomas to establish if it *was* him who was at the receiving end of the incident. I'm sure we will, the house does not go on forever," Scott said.
"I hope he's okay," I said, damn well knowing he wasn't.
"You're not alone," Scott said and tilted his head a little bit to look into the hallway.
"It appears to be a fairly straight shot, my guess is that it came from the centre of the hallway. Was anyone up here right before the shooting?"
"I don't know. I don't think so. I know Thomas went upstairs to sleep. He told me," I said. My nerves started getting higher an higher, I could tell him he did, right? Scott looked back at me and squinted his eyes a little.
"What did the two of you discuss prior to him going upstairs?" He asked.

For a second I was tempted to tell him about Thomas' planned suicide, but I couldn't. He *didn't* kill himself. I

152

couldn't let him get written off as a suicide, even though Marilyn killed him.

"He needed some support, he was hit with his emotions about Nancy," I said.

"Did he seem particularly distraught?" He asked.

"A little, but I suggested he'd get some sleep."

"Ah. Well, the bullet appeared to have hit from a distance further than his own hand could have provided him with, so he either got the trigger pulled on him, or he was the one pulling the trigger on someone else."

"Someone else?"

"It would explain why he is not present, he could have taken the opportunity to flee the scene and take the body with him."

"Do you mean someone outside the people who were here?"

"I do. It could be entirely possible." The story shifted, but not in a way I expected. As long as no one found Thomas it wouldn't hurt anyone else.

"Could he have gone down the stairs to the kitchen?" I asked, adding oil to the fire that was Scott.

"Possibly," Scott pondered, then up and walked towards the stairs I was talking about that were only a couple of feet away. Good thing Marilyn and I took the one further away.

Step by step he examined the stairs. Everything, the steps, the railing, the wall, even the ceiling. I pretended to look as hard as I could too. I knew we wouldn't find anything, nothing related to this at least. These stairs were carpeted in a textured kind of gray fabric. The railings were more like brass than gold, looking close to bronze. No paintings here, thank fuck. No blood or whatever, though. The carpet was a little harsh, it wasn't made like the one

153

upstairs. Every now and then a tint of blueish and blackish spots, more due to age than anything else. Our muffled footsteps sounded throughout the echoey space. Good thing Mari and I didn't take this one, we would've been even louder than we undoubtedly were.

I still was far from sober. Not in the same way I was before, though. I think the death of Thomas changed it. Never had I been so on-edge. All of a sudden I saw a blue spot appear from where Scott had stood next to. Not the same blue spot that appeared every now and then. This one looked familiar.

"Hey, what's that?" I asked and pointed. Scott looked back and then at where I pointed. He bent down and looked at it a little closer.
"Seems to be the same as you found earlier," he said and gestured me to come closer. I did, of course, I got so close I could smell his perfume or whatever they used in this time. It smelled good, dude. I squinted and looked at the blue thing. It was the same cufflink as in the kitchen. 'SS' on it.
"Samuel must've been here," I said. "Maybe when he went up to get a drink before he died."
"Yes, but why would it be here?" Scott asked.
"He might've went into the kitchen first, but when there were no drinks there he went up via the quickest way."
"You may be right," Scott said. "No need to halt our current investigation, we better get on with it. The sooner we find out more the better." Doubtful. Better for him, not for Mari and me. He continued looking intently around him and stepping down the stairs one foot after the other. Soon we came into the kitchen.
"It's curious, no trace of blood anywhere to be found, yet an considerable area of it right above us. It is as if the

154

person has disappeared." He rubbed his neck and stepped a little further into the kitchen. I took a dishtowel and wiped my forehead. I was a little sweaty, probably a combination of nerves and alcohol. Scott's gaze fell on it. "Or as if the wound was bound before taken away. To what end we have yet to figure out, my guess is either to stop the bleeding to get away or in the hope they could help slow down the death and get help in time." All that from a towel? God, he was good. I saw his eyes scan the area like he did in Nancy's room.

"The fastest way to get out would be through the door in the family room, onto the balcony and right off of it on the right, enabling them to slip from the sight of the main window."

Wow, we should've fucking thought of that. Instead Thomas was just out there laying on the other balcony — one I didn't even know existed before I came in, just as I didn't know about the fucking wine cellar. I could've done so much with that.

"But I do not think that is the case here. I believe the body is still around in the building."
"Why?" I asked. Scott smiled.
"I locked the door when I locked the house down and I am in possession of the only key," he said. I laughed a quick laugh.
"Clever," I said.

"If you were to hide a body, where would you hide it?" Scott asked me while we walked through the kitchen toward the big stairs in the main hall. We walked pretty slow, still trying to discover clues. He was, at least. I was trying to guide us away from Thomas' actual location, every second I could stall him was one I took. I tried to drop the guilt I felt but I couldn't help but shiver every time I thought back.

"Maybe somewhere people don't care to look because it seems too obvious," I said. It was the farthest from what Mari and I did, we'd be alright.

"In plain sight, you mean?" He asked.

"Maybe not plain sight but hidden in a spot we're usually at," I said.

"Hm," Scott said and put up his thinking face. Nancy's blood was still by the door of the bathroom, we both didn't mention it. We knew what it was from, it didn't have to do with Thomas. It did, in a way, but not with this case. I felt a little weird investigating my own crime.

"Or somewhere no one would *think* to look. Didn't mrs. Donovan mention the existence of one place that not even mr. Singretti knew of?" Whatever suited him. He wasn't there.

"She did, brilliant idea," I said.

I did feel like a Watson, this must be what Samuel would've felt like in my original story. Not doing any of the real heavy lifting but being there for support and insight. I didn't have all the responsibility, but did get to look around with Scott at the crime. Scott nodded and with a bit of a jog he ran to the opening of the sitting area and stuck his head around the corner.

"Excuse me, mrs. Jones. Where can we find the wine cellar?" He asked.

"Is Nardo alright?" I heard Jack ask.

"He is. Please, mrs. Jones, the cellar?"

"On the opposite side of the hallway to the balcony. There's a door at the end that leads to a big room, you'll find a door next to a staircase that leads upstairs. Open the door and you'll be there," I heard Joan say.

156

"Understood. Thank you." Big room with stairs? Wasn't that where Mari and I—

"Let's go, Berratare," Scott said and walked into the hallway. Oh no we don't. I ran after him. To my horror I saw the door to the balcony where we dropped Thomas off. It wasn't see-through so we couldn't see him, but the fact he was *there* was enough. Scott luckily didn't even acknowledge the door and went straight the the door we also went through.

The big, wooden door to the cellar stood in a doorpost with a rounded top, decorated with wooden vines and grapes. There were a bunch of buttons on either side of the door. They looked a bit liked old light switches or elevator buttons. They were worked into the grape vine design. You couldn't miss it if you tried. How did no one know about the cellar? Seriously, no one even once stumbled upon it during a party?

Scott pulled the door open and went down more stairs that hid behind it. I carefully walked behind him. It was dark on the other side of the door at the bottom of the stairs. The ceiling of the cellar was just a little higher than that door, not connected to the ceiling of the stairs in any way. The top of the door was lower than the bottom of the door we came from, we went down a good twenty feet. The door at the bottom of the stairs was metal. There were holes in it, giving it a grate-like feel.

"Let's look around," Scott said and turned on a light switch, making the entire cellar light up piece by piece. In a flash I saw Thomas sitting against one of the vats, eyes dead set on me with a torn up neck. I blinked a couple times, the next second he was gone. Vats upon vats upon vats were stacked on top of each other, some stuck in the walls. In the walls were probably huge tanks of wine, knowing the count. Some barrels were open but had food in them like cheese or shit like that. Shit that doesn't spoil as quickly. No Thomas, luckily.

"I don't think he's here," I said.
"I'm afraid you're right," I heard Scott say from behind some vats. His head popped up from behind them.
"No trace of anyone." He walked toward me and gestured to the stairs and door. Gentleman. After I was out of the room he switched the light off and followed me.
"There not only was no sight of anyone, neither did I smell or hear anything," Scott pondered.

We walked back into the big room, Scott closed the door to the cellar. I wistfully took a last glance as the doors closed. It would've been useful as hell in my original story. Would've spiced shit up. Not the way this story was going, some non-death spice. We walked back through the other door, the one to the balcony. Scott's head jerked down and he stopped, stretching his arm to stop me from walking further too. He kneeled down and swiped his finger over the floor, then smelled his finger.
"Blood," he said. I looked up from his finger. He stood right in front of the door to the side balcony. Fuck me.

Chapter 11

He swung open the door before I could even think of an excuse why *not* to do exactly that with more power than he swung any other doors before. Not even one step onto the balcony we saw the body. He hesitated but then lunged down next to Thomas and examined his wound. He didn't say a thing, I couldn't see his face, all I saw was Thomas' legs and stomach. And a pool of blood, just as big as the one upstairs if not bigger, though this one was darker than that one was. I heard Scott sniff and clear his throat. Mine was closing up again, without even having seen Thomas' face.

"He's dead," Scott said. Pain shot through my heart. Real pain, it was almost as if a vein snapped.
"Fuck," I said, both about the pain and the confirmation he was *really* dead. "Who could've done something like this?" Scott placed a hand on Thomas' chest.
"Whoever it was committed a heinous crime. He was alive for in the least 15 minutes after he was shot." *What?* "I can see there was an attempt to stop the bleeding to relocate him but as soon as he was, it was taken off and he bled to death," he said. "There was no concern for his recovery, only the cover up."

My heart sank. He was still alive when I laid him outside? He was still alive when we *left him alone on the balcony*? Scott moved to face me, showing Thomas and his wound. My breath escaped and quickened. The hole in the side of Thomas' neck was even worse then I remembered. A little bit frozen over, but drenched in blood like the ground was.

I could've saved him. I could've *fucking* saved him. Scott moved back in front of Thomas' body but kept facing me.

"Do you want to wait outside while I investigate the body?" He asked. I shook my head.
"No, I'm okay. I've just never seen something like this."
"Are you certain you want to stay? If you're uncomfortable with the sight I want to make it abundantly clear you're welcome to wait outside," he said. "I'd much rather you keep a clear head and your sanity than try and stomach it."
"It's fine, it's not the first dead body of the day," I said. But the first I spent a lot of time with. The first with a visible wound, too. Scott's eyes rested on me for another moment, but then nodded and shifted his attention back to Thomas.
"It seems to be the second *planned* murder. We cannot be sure just yet but all signs point to it being that case," he said.
"And the first non-poison one," I said, trying to look anywhere but directly at Thomas.
"Indeed. Do you know if anyone was upstairs right before that very moment?"
"I don't, I can't be sure." I was already copying his lingo.
"Where were you?"

My thoughts raced through my head. Marilyn and I came running out of the sitting room when Jack and Joan came downstairs so I couldn't say I was still in the dining room. I didn't think it was smart to say Marilyn and I were together either, Scott could think there was something going on. There technically wasn't, but him thinking it could be bad for both of us. I could say kitchen, but why would I be there? I was there just before with Jack. He could attest to that. Maybe after the talk with Thomas I felt hungry again and went back for more. It was my best bet, Scott already knew the 'killer' didn't go through there. Fuck, but I would've said it before when we were investigating in the kitchen if I was there when the murder happened. Maybe the balcony? But why would I stand with three dead bodies? Willingly? Maybe to contemplate about Thomas' words after he told me he was suicidal. Did I want to throw Thomas under the bus like that, though? *I've* murdered him, not he himself. Did I have that much of an other option though? Jack and Joan knew we weren't in the sitting area with them. Besides, Scott already said it couldn't have been a suicide. The angle of the bullet and all of that.

"I was at the balcony, I had to clear my head after Thomas and I talked. The other balcony," I said. I felt a wave of guilt while Thomas laid on the ground, dead.
"Oh? Do explain, please." I hesitated. Did I actually wanna go there?
"Well," I started. Scott nodded encouragingly. "He wasn't feeling too good. He talked to Marilyn just before, I discovered it was to mend their relationship before he—," I stopped. I couldn't get it out of my mouth. Scott took the hint, though.
"I see," he said and went silent for a second. The roar of the snowstorm took over the balcony. It was still way too fucking cold for my liking, but it wasn't nearly as bad in this suit.
"For what it's worth, I can reassure you. It wasn't him who pulled the trigger. For one, his body would've stayed upstairs. Instead, he had his wound wrapped and was taken here, something someone with this type of wound surely wouldn't be able to do." He turned to Thomas' body as if he got a thought.

"What's more is that the wound cover was later removed, you can see the mark of it still on his neck," he said and pointed to Thomas' neck. There was a red band of a straight lined stripe around his neck.

"The material has soaked up the blood, then colored his neck more red on that specific part. The material has been removed but the mark is still there. He wouldn't have bound it if it a suicide to begin with, let alone *taken it off.*" He looked back at me with a smile.

"I didn't put those points together before. That's very good," he said.

"Yeah, very good," I repeated. Fuck me. I doubted it was. For Marilyn and me, at least. How did I get him to this when I was actively trying to *prevent* him getting there? My sadness for Thomas turned into fear.

"What leaves us to do now is look for signs of the material, perhaps we can pinpoint it to a person. What would be a place you would discard evidence if you had done what was done to Thomas?" He asked.

"I would make sure no one would find it, preferably destroying it," I said and looked at the edge of the balcony where it was a straight cliff down to death. The mansion stood on a mountain slash cliff, this balcony probably hanging over it the most of the entire house.

"Do you think the murderer threw it down there?" Scott asked. I nodded.

"Hmm, perhaps. We won't find it in that case, that's for certain. As with all, however, that is just one of the options. We'll search for it nonetheless. By the way, I must say that I like that suit. I suits you well," he said and turned around, kneeling to look underneath a couch. I froze. The suit. I forgot about the suit.

"Right, thank you," I said, kneeling down too and I looked underneath a statue.

Did he suspect me? Was that why he wanted me around? To try and get me to confess? Talking about 'where would you hide those things' and seeing if I would accidentally snitch on myself? It obviously worked, he found the body. And I was out here thinking he wanted me to be the Watson to his Sherlock. No, I was the Moriarty to his Sherlock instead. Difference was that I wasn't as smart as Moriarty, that guy would've seen through that shit way earlier. What would Scott do when he found out?

I frowned. Couple of roaches but no bloody rag. Good thing I at least told her to not leave it on his neck.

What *would* he do? Worst thing that could happen is that he would keep me locked in his side office until police came, but I would probably — hopefully — already be gone when that happened. That would be *worst case* scenario. All I had to fear besides that was poison if that shit was still around, but since Samuel drank some and destroyed the rest of it by dropping it on the ground, there was almost no way I would get poisoned or die. Unless Marilyn would shoot me too, but there'd be no chance.

I crawled to a big chair and looked underneath it. Nothing, obviously. The cold of the stones creeped into my hands and knees. Next time I gotta get stuck inside a story with warmth. I put my hands together and blew in them. It didn't help, I barely still felt anything.

"Are you cold?" I heard from behind me.
"A little bit, yeah."
"We'd better get inside then. Besides, I see the chance of us finding any additional clues here very low. This is merely the place he was discarded. I've seen what I

needed to see." I stood up and turned around to face him. I shivered, Thomas was laying only a few feet away from me.

"Do you think it was me?" I asked.

"It was you who did what, exactly? There's been quite a few instances tonight."

"Kill him," I said. To my surprise Scott smiled a quick smile as he led me inside.

"No, mister Berratare, I do not. Though I know you weren't on the balcony when Thomas was shot. I do not know for what reason you would withhold the truth but my suspicion is not on you. That's why I asked you along." He closed the door to the balcony and put his hand on my shoulder.

"If I even had the slightest suspicion that you *did* have something to do with the death of Thomas, I would not ask you along. I would question you like I did before any of these new situations unfolded in the beginning of the evening."

"Okay, then what are we going to do now?" I asked.

"We will look for the bloodied material. As of right now that is our priority." He paused. "No, excuse me, first thing I'll do now is use the restroom. If you don't mind," he said and walked past me to the bathroom.

"Here? Isn't this one old?" I asked in a half-assed attempt to stop him.

"Trust me when I tell you it works perfectly fine," he said. Right, he was there with Marilyn when I came into the story.

I sighed and right after yawned. Well, I tried. I leaned my shoulder against the wall on the other side of the door to the balcony. The tiredness crept up on me, I felt empty and tired. Why did I get fucked up over Thomas the way I did? I knew him for all of one evening. He wasn't actually

164

dead. He'd be alive every time the story starts over. So would all the others, except the count. He'd always be dead, as he deserved. It wouldn't be long until Scott would find Marilyn's dress and the piece out of it. Maybe he didn't know it was hers. But Joan probably would. Fuck all of them. Fuck this story. It got me in mindsets I didn't like. I got too sucked into it, even though I was quite literally sucked into it. And sucked off in it. I wasn't even sober for most of it. I was a fucking alcoholic, as were all of these people. Besides Scott. And Joan maybe, I didn't remember her drinking much if at all. Maybe that's why I liked her better than Jessica. A better influence on people. If I ever got out of this shit I had to start drinking less. I knew I was an alcoholic. I think that thought made me do it more, drinking myself deeper and deeper into self-pity. Murder mystery turned therapy. Who would've thought.

The toilet flushed and I heard the tap running, for washing his hands probably. I heard the rolling of paper out of the dispenser, his foot on the trashcan opener. The door opened with the same force as he opened all doors and his head peeped around the corner. He nodded me to come over.

"You're not naked, are you?" I asked.
"This is far more serious." He held up the trashcan and showed me the inside. I saw the paper towels laid down on the washing table, he hadn't put them in the trashcan. Instead, the black velvet dress. He picked it out of the trashcan and revealed the bloody scrap of dress on the bottom underneath it. I tried to look as shocked as I could. "The material," I said. "Wow, that was quick." He nodded and took it out.

"It appears to belong to the dress that was put on top of it. There's a considerable piece missing from it, as big as the material itself is."

"Do you know who's dress it is?" I asked. I hoped for Marilyn that he didn't. Though he was her date, so maybe the consequences would be less bad if he found out she killed Thomas.

"Marilyn's."

"Marilyn?"

"Additionally, she is in the possession of a gun. If it matches the bullet that was used, we will have found who murdered Thomas."

"You knew she had a gun? Why didn't you question her first?" I asked.

"It's rather embarrassing, I would appreciate it if you didn't tell anyone. I simply didn't want to believe it was her, so I put it aside. Additionally I did not know what type of gun hers is, so I figured it could be a coincidence. I see now that that was unwise."

Not for Marilyn, though now he knew anyway. God damn it Marilyn, telling every guy you hang out with you have a gun. Not very effective. That way if they turn on you, they'll already know.

"No I get it, man. You wanted to protect her."

"I shouldn't have let it made me blind to the truth. All evidence points to her," he replied.

"Marilyn is a blessing and a curse," I said.

I should know, I helped her cover up a body. Not successfully, but I helped her nonetheless. I could've let her handle it alone but I was the one that told her to shoot the vase. While drunk. I genuinely was the reason this story went to shit. All the deaths beside Nancy and the count were thanks to me. I *was* the villain of the story. It wasn't even intentional, that's what was worse. I could be an amazing villain if it was intentional but here I was, crying over my characters. Scott didn't reply, instead he was staring at the bloody dress piece.

"What's the next move?" I asked.
"An interrogation, I suppose. We do not yet have all the facts. As of right now she is not aware of our knowledge of the situation. This can greatly benefit us."
"How?"
"The answers will be untainted by fear." No the fuck they wouldn't. She knew I knew she knew. I was there, and now with Scott. Helping with the investigation — not planned, but I ended up getting him the answers anyway. I handed them on a gold platter.

"Everyone's still here, that's a first," I said while walking into the sitting area.
"The less of us are alive, the less courageous the rest of us get," Jack mumbled and looked up to me. "Glad to see you're alright, Nardo. What did you two find?" Scott walked past me trough the archway and positioned himself in front of Marilyn, Joan and Jack.
"Not quite enough. I need some of you for questioning. Worry not, it'll be the same as we did at the start of the evening. I would like to start with Marilyn," he said. Marilyn tensed up but her face showed nothing. Wish I could do that. Imagine what you could do with that.
"Okay," she said.
"Do you need me in there or can I stay here?" I asked. Figured I might as well ask, me being the Watson of the story.
"No, that's alright." He swooped into the side room, closely followed by Marilyn.

I sat down on one of the leather chairs and moved my fingertips over the smooth but sturdy leather. Was bit wrinkly in some parts, it reminded me of my grandmother's chair. The sense of real-ness spread through my fingertips into my hands and arms. I sighed and put my hand on my chest. My mind was a bit clearer than it was before. Joan and Jack were the quietest they'd been the entire evening too, probably just as worn out. Should I care about these people dying? They weren't real, but it damn sure felt like they were. I knew them for months even though I met them just this night. I didn't even fucking like most of them when I wrote them, now there was a dead body that used to be a friend every fucking hour.

"*Did* you find something?" Jack asked after a while. His gaze at me, but if I didn't know any better he could just as well be looking right through me.
"I found the wine cellar, does that count?"
"That's good I suppose, perhaps Thomas isn't dead."

A wave of just pure distraught came over me. It was like his name was a trigger. It probably was, trauma wise. I wasn't stupid. I knew this shit was gonna have an impact, world being real or not didn't matter. I still went through it. Why the fuck did I need to write a mystery novel.

"He is the only one not present," Joan said. "We heard a gunshot, Jack. We *saw*—" she didn't finish her sentence. Imagine if I knew these people for as long as they knew each other. I couldn't, to be fair. I didn't have a group of friends or family as big as these guys. I had that guy that worked for my publishers, I knew him since high school. I knew Jess, but she wasn't in my life anymore. I had a bunch of people I knew beside that but none I considered

168

friends. Family wasn't any better. I had my parents but I knew none of my family on my mom's side, my dad's were all dead. I guess I could see my parents dying as a similar thing to what happened here, if that guy and some other people died too. Mate, I'd have no one left.

"We don't know yet," I said with a slight shake in my voice. I tried to hide it by coughing, but no one seemed to notice anyway. Jack nodded along and looked back into the night.
"We do not," he concluded. Joan looked down.
"What time is it anyway," I asked. Jack shook his arm to get his watch to face him and squinted a little.
"Around three," he said.
"Jesus, when did this evening start?"
"I believe eight or so, though the real party started around nine or ten."
"The real party being—," I started.
"Yes. That party," Jack replied. Joan scoffed.
"It isn't a party. When is it going to end? This evening has been dragging out for hours and all of us are tired and shaken up. I genuinely don't think I can do this for any longer."
"Just hold tight for a little longer, Joan. It's going to end sooner or later. Let the detective do his thing and maybe we will find out tonight what it is and maybe we won't, but we can't stop it now," Jack said. Joan sighed a desperate sigh and looked away.
"I want to find out who's been killing all these people. Until we know, we can't be sure that we are safe," he went on.
"Yes, and that's the worst thing. We *do not know if we are safe*. Why would we stay here when we can't be certain we will stay alive?"

"I'm sure we will be fine. We stayed alive for the biggest part of the evening so far, I don't think it's likely that we will die," I said.

"Sure, but there's another death, we don't even know who it is. No, actually, we do. Thomas is the only one not here. Thomas is dead. I didn't think he was going to pass away either. But here we are, my uncle's dead, Samuel's dead, Nancy's dead and now him too. It's been only five hours and *four* people have died."

"I know, but—,"

"How long before another person dies. How long before I die? I don't want to die."

She started tearing up but quickly wiped it away with her hand.

"I just got him back a year and a half ago," she said. Jack put his arm around her but she brushed him away and stood up.

"Whether or not he is dead, Thomas was right. I'm going to bed," she said and walked away barely hiding her tears. Jack stood up and attempted to follow her.

"Alone," she said without looking back. Jack stopped in his tracks and stood still with his arms by his side, seemingly unsure of what to do. He looked back at me with a questioning face. I nodded my head to the couch. Probably best that she got some sleep, Marilyn and I weren't upstairs this time after all. No one to shoot her or murder her.

"Let her go," I said. After one last look at Joan — who was already halfway up the stairs — he turned around and sat back down on the couch.

"Mate, this is awful," he said. I just nodded. It was.

I could still see Thomas' face as he got shot. Clear as day. I could see his face as he went limp in my hands. His face on the balcony, his wound exposed to the cold. Jack and

Joan's voices after we ran away with him. I could feel his head dangle on my back, his feet and legs on my chest and thighs. I could feel the pouring of his blood on my hands when I tried to keep him alive. Which he was, as it turned out. He was alive for 15 minutes after the shot. *Fifteen. Fifteen more minutes.*

"What did Scott want with you before?" Jack asked.
"He wanted my help." Jack frowned.
"Why's that?"
"He said we were on the same page a lot. That I was accurate in a lot of situations."
"Like the poison?" He asked. I nodded.
"Yeah, like the poison."
"And, did you help?"
"Unexpectedly, yeah." Jack raised his eyebrows as if to say he needed more than that.
"Well?" He asked. I didn't know if I could talk about Thomas being dead.
"We found some things."
"Like?"
"Another one of those cufflinks. Same color, same initials."
"Samuel's? Where'd you find that?"
"The stairs by the kitchen," I replied.
"Huh," Jack said and stared into the dark of the night.
"I heard about your company, by the way. I saw the paper on Stonier's desk. I'm sorry he was an ass," I said to fill the silence. Jack waved it away.
"Compared to everything else that happened the last few weeks it's nothing," he said.
"Didn't it lose you a lot of money?" I asked. Jack sighed.
"Mate, I have more than enough money. Enough to sustain a hundred people ten lifetimes over. I don't care about money, I'd rather have the people back that I lost," he said.

"I get that," I replied. "Your dad, right?" I asked. He nodded and clearly made an attempt to keep his face straight. I sighed, scooted closer to him and put my arm around him. He smelled almost as nice as Scott did.
"Do you want to talk about it?" I asked.
"I'm fine, mate. Don't worry," he said.
"No you ain't," I said. "No one here is." He looked me in the eye for a second and then looked back down.
"Nothing much to say, he killed himself," Jack started. "The worst thing is he told me why in a note," he said, still looking down.
"That's rough, like a suicide note?" I asked.
"I suppose. I just don't know what to do with it," he said. He paused for a second. "It makes all of tonight come in harder."
"Why's that?" I asked.

Maybe he meant just the death, tonight were even more deaths. Deaths upon deaths after losing your father must be rough. Marilyn had the same experience, essentially, except that she didn't have a couple of weeks to mourn before this shit.

"Well—," Jack started with an unsteady voice. He cleared his throat and tried again. "He had an affair with my mother."
"Your father?"
"Stonier."
"Stonier?" Jack just nodded and looked me in the eye.
"Jesus fucking Christ mate," I said. What the fuck. What kind of fucking asshole. Raping Nancy, having affairs with married women, all stacked upon the countless horrible things he had done that weren't even sexual.
"They had one before, years and years ago, before I was even born. My father managed to forgive her then, on the

172

promise she would never do it again. She didn't keep that promise."

Stonier killed a man by sleeping with his wife — twice. He killed a woman by making her pregnant. Everyone who fucked stonier (or had their wife fuck him) died. Even he did. Come to think of it, Marilyn's mother was dead too.

"I couldn't look at my mother the same ever since," he said.
"That's awful mate," I said. He sat up and reached for a glass of alcohol, already half empty, but he didn't seem to care.
"Don't even say it," he said and brought it to his lips. In one gulp it was gone.
"I don't blame you," I said. He put the glass back and sat back down. He rested his head on my shoulder.
"God, how many more hours of this crap," he said.
I picked up the rose I gave Thomas now hours ago that was still laying on the table. I breathed deeply and tried to still my shaky hand. Jack put his hand on mine and took the rose with his other.
"Are *you* okay, mate?" He asked.
"Thomas is dead," I said.

Chapter 12

"I figured as much," Jack said as he laid the rose beside him. He was surprisingly calm. If it wasn't me who killed him he'd be suspicious as fuck. "After a pool of blood as big as that it's hard to think otherwise."

"It looked horrible, I've never seen anything like it and I hope I never will again," I said.

"Where is he?" Jack asked.

"On the smaller balcony," I said. "Close to the wine cellar."

"How the hell did he get there? That's a long way from where we found the blood," He pondered. I shrugged and tried to get Jack and Joan's yells out of my head.

"Scott said he was dumped there." Worst thing was that he was. We just left him there. Scott and I did too. We didn't move him to the other balcony. Maybe because this crime scene was outside in the cold already, I didn't know.

"His neck was blown to bits," I said.

"Bloody hell, good thing Joan is upstairs, with this on top of all that happened I don't know how she would react," Jack said.

"Bad," I replied.

"As anyone would," he paused. "He's with Nancy now." I nodded. I didn't believe in life after death, but that thought was nice.

"Hope so," I said. "That would—," the door of the side room swung open before I could finish my sentence.

Scott looked around the room and then fixed his gaze on me. He gestured me to come over while Marilyn walked out. I raised my eyebrows and pointed at myself. He nodded and gestured once more. I threw a quick look at Jack.

"Good luck," he said and patted my shoulder.

Scott closed the door and sat down on his desk.

"Do you want me to sit down?" I asked.

"If you desire to do so, yes, but it's not necessary," he said.

"Alright," I leaned against the wall. "What did you find out?"

"We were correct. She confessed to murdering Thomas."

She did?

"She did?"

"She did." Fuck.

"What did she say?"

"She murdered Thomas by accident, she told me she was aiming for a vase. Two accidents, both Thomas and Nancy. I am inclined to think neither were legitimate accidents."

At least she didn't snitch on me, I guess. She made herself look a whole lot worse though. "What do you think?"

"Me?" I asked. He nodded. "I haven't spoken to her, so I don't want to come to rash conclusions."

"You are very right," he said and stood up, then gestured to his papers that were at least tripled since I last set foot in his office. I could do nothing but raise my eyebrows. "You sure?"

"I am, Leonardo. I value your opinion and trust your judgement."

Man, when I tell you I have never blushed as hard as I did right then and there. My detective version self trusted me enough to see his work. I shuffled closer to the desk and picked up a paper. He had descriptions of tiny details in body language along with sentences she'd said. 'I didn't mean to, it was an accident, tried shooting vase instead' along with 'C' with an arrow pointing at the text.

175

"What's C?" I asked.

"Confession. Excuse me, there's some abbreviations in the papers. Don't hesitate to ask whenever something is unclear." I nodded and looked at another paper. It was a report of Jack's first questioning, right after the count died. I rustled trough some papers, more and more names popped up. Interesting, I could just do my research on my story right here and now. I got to know most of them on my own now, but it was still useful.

Jack Donovan

Place of residency
I have houses in London, the alps, the Americas and Paris but live mostly in London.
Occupancy
My father's company and a few sister establishments
How would he describe himself
I'm a successful man, one might say handsome, I'm charismatic and fairly wealthy
What does he believe in
Money doesn't buy happiness but sure makes misery easier to live with.
What haunts him
My everlasting hunt for success and recognition.
Height/weight
6'0 feet and 170 lbs
Eye colour
Green
Hair color
Black/very dark brown
What clothing style does he wear
The colour black, however I do like some gray or earth tones once in a while.

Greatest strength
Leadership
Greatest weakness
Temper
Greatest fear
Drowning or not being able to breath otherwise

Seemed about right. Was taken before the other deaths, he still had a bit of sass in him.
"Do you have mine too?" I asked.
"I do, but there won't be anything you aren't yet aware of in there." I put the paper back on the table.
"Judging by that confession I think it was an accident, but I don't know what else you want me to read," I said.
"There's a *lot* of paper and only so much time. Did you find out more about her gun?"
"I inquired about the gun before she confessed to the murder, she confirmed the type of gun she is in possession of. It matches the bullet perfectly. Unfortunately I could not get her to tell me where she hid it, but it'll be a matter of time."
"That seems like pretty solid evidence," I said.
"Indeed, now the question remains if she murdered sir Stonier and indirectly mister Singretti along with the two known deaths by her hand."
"How do we do that?"
"Have you found any — sincerely, any — motives this night? I've seen you around everyone, to my knowledge you've spoken to all suspects."

I didn't immediately speak. It was a bit of a dilemma. I could snitch the people out who told me things probably assuming I wouldn't go around telling Scott, but on the other hand I was really fucking curious who did it. The

177

original murder, that is. The other deaths meant more to me emotion wise but that one had an almost legendary status, I've worked on it for months and still know nothing. No, actually, I do know more. That's why there's a dilemma in the first place.

"I think I got the same you got," I said. Which wasn't that incriminating. This shit with Jack's dad and all of that good trauma inducing material however, don't think Scott would take it that well.
"Do you want to speak to Marilyn? Perhaps you can form your own opinion on it." I raised my brows.
"You want me to talk to Mari?" I asked. He nodded. Officially Watson.
"Yeah, sure. Yeah, where do I talk to her?" I asked.
"Here is fine, I'll send her in. Thank you, Leonardo," he said with a smile and left the room, leaving a wave of his cologne. He had a very nice smile. Was I attracted to that? I don't know, man. I wasn't sure of anything here. The door creaked open and Marilyn slipped inside, very obviously worried.

"What did he tell you?" She asked.
"He thinks you killed Thomas and Nancy, both intended," I said with a grimace. She plopped down in the chair.
"Shit," she murmured, then looked up. "I see you've upgraded."
"He trusts me, yeah. I think that's a good thing."
"Clearly, you've led him to Thomas and got me accused of two murders. Accused of intentionally doing it, I mean. It's not even true, that's the worst part," she said. I sighed and sat down on the desk like Scott had often done before. Guess I really had upgraded.
"It's not ideal, but what would you have me do? I'm still not in the best mindset, but when he approached me I was

going through that shit. I tried my hardest to keep him away."

"Well, you're terrible at it. I would say no offense, but I'm not in a position where I can mean it."

"Yeah, yeah. I get it."

"Shit, Nardo! What the hell do I do now?" She said.

"He said he trusts my opinion, maybe I can convince him you *did* do it by accident," I said. "Why the fuck did you tell him about your gun anyway, by the way?"

"I told you too, stupid."

"Maybe don't, in the future. What do you have it for if everyone knows you've got it?"

"Yes father, I've learned my lesson, thanks."

"Where'd you hide it?"

"I'm not gonna say," she said. "Learned my lesson, remember? For all I know you killed my father."

"Why would I do that? I don't even have a motive."

"Yes you do. Everyone here does. That I don't know it doesn't mean it isn't there."

"So you've got a motive too?"

"Yeah, what do you think? He wasn't the sweetest guy. He killed my god damn mother."

"Fuck, are you serious?" I asked.

"I am," she replied.

"Why are you telling me? You know I've been working with Scott."

"You know damn well you can't say shit. If you so much as utter a word to him about it, I'll tell him you're the reason I shot Thomas." I scoffed.

"Right. Convenient. Sorry about your mom," I said. See, anyone who slept with that bastard died. "How did it happen?"

"Do you really want to know?" She asked. I nodded.

"Well, after he caught her with a valet guy, he bashed her head into the sidewalk and threw his bottle of whiskey at

179

her. She died on impact," she paused. "The valet guy wasn't so lucky. The man got shot in both his legs so he couldn't run away and then got beat to death by my father's bare hands."

"Jesus Christ, you *saw* that shit?" This explained a lot about Marilyn. No offense, of course.

"I did. I was seven."

"Fuck," I said and rubbed my chin. "Well, there's your motive."

"Told you. Now, what's your thing?"

"I don't have a 'thing'," I said.

"Come on Nardo, everyone has a 'thing' with my father."

"If you tell me where the gun is," I said.

"Why do you want to know? Who are you trying to shoot?" I sighed and threw my hands into the air.

"No one, Marilyn. I'm trying to figure shit out. Would you let me, please? I'm tired of this fucking night, I'm just trying to go home with as little trauma as possible." If I got home at all. I hoped I could.

"I'm not gonna tell you, stupid. You told me I needed to learn my lesson. I did. Move on. What are you gonna tell Scott?"

"That you're clinically insane."

"Mister funny man. Seriously, what are we going to do?"

"I'll say I think you did it by accident."

"Thank you," she said and looked down.

"Shit's going to be alright, Marilyn," I said.

"Fool Scott, not me," she said. She stood up and stroked my cheek. "Good luck, love." She walked out of the room. This was something I knew I was attracted to.

"Enlighten me," Scott said after he closed the door.

"I think she did it, but by accident," I said. She did, no lie there.

"Yes? What led you to come to that conclusion?"

180

"The very obvious lack of motive first of all. They had some trouble after Nancy but they resolved it completely, actually right before his death."

"I assume you've heard of a pre-suicide high?" He started. I nodded. That's probably why Thomas made up with Mari, but not why she was gonna want to shoot him.

"Perhaps she had already made up her mind and so went along with anything he told her. A reverse pre-suicide high, if you will."

"You mean she was agreeing with his shit because she knew she was going to kill him anyway?" I asked. This time *he* nodded.

"Isn't that a little far-fetched? She looked genuinely relieved after their talk."

"It's more common than you might think in my line of work," he said. "But, I value your point of view and I will take it along in my report. Did you come across anything else?" You could say that, yeah. Some good old childhood trauma.

"It's hard to make out what's important and what's not," I said. "There has been so much going on. I have to be honest, I wasn't fully sober for a big part of the night."

"I'm aware," Scott said, his face was still kind of unreadable but I saw a hint of amusement. "And it's understandable. There's been a considerable amount of death tonight, more than you likely bargained for when you started today." I didn't expect to come here at all, to be fair.

"I do have to ask you to look through your memories for anything that may be important, nonetheless."

I bit my lip. I realized I didn't want any of them to get ratted out. Even if one of them did it. The only reason I still wanted to know who did it besides Thomas was

181

because I needed to put a story on paper in the real world and I just genuinely got curious to who finally killed the motherfucker. No one of the people still here had bad reasons to kill him. Joan had maybe the least convincing one, but still pretty valid reasons to kill over. Mate, Jack and Marilyn though. A different story. Leonardo probably had some shit going on with the count too, some shit I didn't even know about. Scott didn't even know any of us before tonight. Good introduction to the family, he definitely got to know them.

"Joan was about to be taken out of the will," I said. Better play it safe, I didn't know what he knew or didn't.
"Was she now?" He asked. Let me rephrase that. Played it stupid, I didn't know what he knew or didn't.
"You didn't know?" I asked.
"I did not, no." Ah, come one. This was the safest thing I could've said. He grabbed his notepad and wrote it down.
"Well, now you know," I said. "Do you know Samuel and the count had a big fight a week or so ago?"
"That's very interesting. I didn't, no." I didn't either, I wasn't even here back then. "But I was referring more to any of the more recent deaths, specifically Thomas. I have multiple leads for sir Stonier and Nancy, but Singretti and Thomas are slightly more abstract. We know Marilyn murdered Thomas, but we, as of yet, do not know the reasoning behind it—," Scott said. I interrupted him.
"What's going to happen to Marilyn anyway?"
"Likely some form of punishment, but that's only when the police arrives in the morning. For now we have very limited options."
"Yeah, I guess you're right. There's not much you can do here."

"Indeed. But, if it starts to genuinely bother you we can surely think of something," he said. Did he think I was scared of Marilyn?

"Alright, maybe later," I said. Scott nodded.

"That's it for now, as long as you do not have any additional information. I'll spare you the going over the details, I'll need just a moment."

"Just yell whenever you need me," I replied and opened the door.

Yelling there was, Marilyn and Jack seemed to be wrapped in what looked like a fight.

"Hey, what's going on?" I asked and jogged to the sitting area. "Nardo, how did it go?" Jack asked, now completely disregarding Marilyn. Marilyn threw a magazine at him.

"He's Scott's left hand now," she said. Jack dodged the magazine.

"I'm aware, he told me," He said. I tilted my head for a second and sighed, then sat down next to him.

"He trusts me, for some reason. Be honest, do I look trustworthy?" Jack pretended to examine me very carefully. I laughed and rolled my eyes. Goofball.

"No, no I don't think so," Jack said. "What do you think, Marilyn? No, wait, I don't care. Never mind."

"Ass," she murmured.

"Both of you trusted me though, never knew I was that inviting," I said.

"You're alright, Nardo. I know you would never put me in a compromising situation with the things I told you," he said.

"I wouldn't, but it does make it hard around Scott," I said.

"I knew you were gay," Marilyn grinned.

"It doesn't make *that* hard around Scott, you get what I mean," I replied.

"I do, I appreciate it," Jack said.

"You told him what you said you would, right?" Marilyn asked. I nodded.

"What did you tell him to tell Scott?" Jack asked.

"I hardly think that concerns you," Marilyn replied.

"In an evening as this it does, most certainly. Get over yourself, Marilyn." We really couldn't use this tension.

"Scott was on Mari's ass about Nancy, she asked me to say she didn't do it on purpose," I said. Half truth is better than a lie.

"He's still on that crap? I understand it's a serious thing but there's been two more deaths since," Jack said.

"Hey, I think I'm gonna get Joan, she's slept for a little bit now. I think it's best if we all keep an eye on each other," I said.

"Ah, you're right. Would probably for the better," Jack said.

"Let the woman sleep," Marilyn said.

"No, I'm gonna get her," I said. "See the two of you in a bit. Don't move, aye?"

"See you in a bit, Nardo," Jack said and grabbed the magazine Marilyn had thrown at him. He didn't seem to enjoy it, but kept reading anyway.

"Well, hurry back," Marilyn said. "I don't think it's a good idea."

"Yeah, you've made that clear, Marilyn. Put a sock in it," Jack said.

I walked up the steps, no click clacking shoes this time. I was a little concerned about Marilyn and Jack, but more than that I was concerned about how Joan was holding up. We hadn't seen her in a bit. Last time that happened someone died.

The balustrade that continued on all through the side of the other steps was partially hidden by the thick red drapes that were slightly more closed now, the golden

184

ropes dangled around, no longer having a purpose. The big pots with roses were still as bushy as before. It didn't hit as good as it did before. I picked a rose from the pot and smelled it. Still real. Bizarre, to be fair. That was a fuck ton of roses to keep alive or change out for fresh ones. I put it back with it's friends and walked into the east wing.

"Joan?" I said to the empty hallway. I walked slower and slower. I already saw *that* spot. A bit of red peeped around the corner. I turned around out of instinct, but didn't walk back. God, fuck Marilyn for shooting him in the east wing. I closed my eyes and pinched the bridge of my nose. Close your eyes, you'll be there soon. I took a step backwards. I understood what Thomas meant earlier when we tried to go into the kitchen now. I understood why he wanted to get the fuck out. Now it was him who was dead, and me who didn't wanna go. And we weren't even married.

I slowly opened one eye and peeked backwards to see if I was walking into something. A trauma trap, but no walls, luckily. Marilyn was right, this wasn't that good of an idea. I shuffled backwards, one foot after the other in the direction of Joan's room.

"Joan?" I said again. I inhaled sharply and ran around the corner. A dark red stain on the carpet blew me right against the wall, looking at it like it was a thousand foot drop into a ravine. Head slightly tilted upwards while looking down, fear of death, all that good shit.

"Joan?" I asked another time. Arms spread out against the wall like I was trying to prove I had a big span width I shuffled sideways through the hall, trying to look anywhere but the red black hole that somehow sucked my gaze into it.

"Joan?" I said. I closed my eyes. Relying fully on touch I shuffled on, bump on the wall after bump. Finally, a doorpost and a handle. I pushed it down like my life depended on it — even though it very much *did not* — and stumbled inside. Joan sat up in her bed, disgruntled and all.

"Nardo, what are you doing?" She grumbled. I pushed the door closed and leaned against it.
"Good morning, sunshine," I said. "I'm getting you to go downstairs." I sank down to the floor, trying to catch a breath.
"How the fuck did you get past that giant blood stain?" I asked.
"My feet have been walking me since I was a child," she said. "Why do we need to go down? Is Thomas found?"
Fuck, I forgot she didn't know yet.
"Eh, yeah, so to speak," I said. She got a concerned look on her face. Rightfully so, I was being weird as hell.
"Is he—," she asked. I bit my lip. She pulled her blanket over her head.
"When is it going to end?" She exclaimed.
"Scott is on the right path," I said. "Don't worry, we'll get there soon."
"That's what you said hours ago," she said with a muffled, shaky voice.
"And it's what I'll keep saying. We're still, alive, right?" I said. "It must be working."
"Did you tell Thomas the same thing?" I stared at the blankets.
"Yes," I said and walked up to the pile.

"Can I sit down?" I asked. The pile went up and down. Could be interpreted as either, but I sat down anyway. I awkwardly put a hand on the pile. I hadn't done anything like this in a long time. With Jess, at least.

"I know I can't promise no one else will die, but I will do my best to try and make sure you won't." A head popped up from the pile of blankets.

"It's so bleak," she said. Tear stripes ran down her cheeks. I carefully wiped some away with my fingers.

"I know, I wish we could leave this night behind. But we can't, so the next best thing is to all stay together so no one else dies." She looked at me for a second with her big eyes.

"We can stay here for a couple of minutes if you want, but I do want to get down after," I said. She nodded and laid back down, staring at the ceiling.

"I did *not* expect tonight to unfold this way," she said. I laid down next to her and sighed.

"Me neither."

Chapter 13

"I loved you," I said to the silent room. "We've seen each other only at parties. How can you love me?"

"Not love, loved. And not you, technically. You just look an awful lot like my ex."

"Like your ex? What are you going on about?" She asked.

"Yeah, and Jack looks like the guy my ex is with now," I said.

"Are you going mad?" She asked.

"Likely."

"Alright," she said. She paused for a second. "What was your ex like, then?"

"Well, she was very beautiful. She was like you at first, but she became more and more of a bitch as time passed."

"Why's that?"

"I don't know, I didn't even notice it at first. We were together for a few years, but you — she, I mean, cheated on me. Sorry, you didn't."

"Oh, that's tough. What was her name?"

"Jessica."

"Ha, a J name too."

"Coincidentally yeah."

"Tell me more about your relationship," she said. I sighed.

"I met her at a party, we were both *very* drunk, but I knew immediately she was what I was looking for. I was a writer back then too," I started.

"You are a writer? I thought you were in business," she interrupted.

"I write too."

"Are you any good?" She asked.

"I like to think so, yeah. I won a lot of things when I was younger and I got a lot of attention from it. Anyway, we danced together that entire evening and we woke up in her house the next morning. I had work, so I showed up in work in a shirt of hers, I lost mine and couldn't find it in time. We lost contact for a while because I forgot to ask for her number," I said.

"Telephone number?"

"Yeah, telephone number. Our luck was good though, I saw her in a grocery store about a week and a half later. She had to leave, but gave me her number. I still had your shirt, after all."

"Right, she had to have that back."

"Naturally. So, we went out on a real date, I showed up in her shirt, she in mine. We didn't plan it, we both thought it would be funny. It was a really good date. We woke up in my house this time."

"Ah, need to keep it fresh, of course. Some new things every now and then," she said.

"Exactly. We kept dating and after six months she moved in with me because I lived closer to the museum she really wanted to work at. She got the job, I visited a lot in the beginning."

"What happened next?"

"Well, I guess we grew apart. She used to give me amazing stories to use in my writing from the museum, but after a while it became routine. I stayed home more often because she didn't want me to go out partying when she had an early shift. She didn't hang out with your friends as much anymore, they had jobs and she did too. I worked at home."

"Sounds like it hit a dead end," Joan said.

"It did for her, I think. She said she didn't want me to come to the museum anymore, supposedly because her tours got busier and busier, but it ended up being because she was cheating on me in the museum."

"How did you find out?"

"I came to surprise her one day on her job because she had a rough week, came in with flowers and a box of chocolate. The receptionist says she wasn't on a tour, which she said she was, I find her in a broom closet fucking this guy," I said.

"That's awful," Joan replied. "That must've been a horrible feeling."

"The worst."

"It makes sense why you're the way you are now, I have to say. I think you just put all of your attention to her," Joan said. "How did your writing go after she left and didn't have any stories for you?"

Look at this story and you have your answer. I didn't reply.

"Your writing fell short because you gave all of your attention to her."

"Yeah, maybe you're right," I replied.

"There's always two sides to a story. Maybe she didn't feel happy in the relationship anymore."

"Yeah, I actually saw the two of them earlier this morning. I thought they two took me somewhere after I got drunk because you look so much like her." She didn't respond right away.

"Must have been weird to see me walk in on you and Marilyn kiss then," she then said. I opened my mouth but closed it again. I just nodded.

"I'm glad you like Mari though. Does she remind you of anyone?"

"No, only you two. Besides Scott, I already knew him before today. Sort of."

She laughed again and laid down on my chest. My breath calmed down and I looked at her. She didn't notice, it was still dark in the room. Her soft hair touched my chin a little. Weird, it's how Jess was back when we just met. Even weirder was that I didn't feel anything. For her, I didn't feel anything for her anymore. I scoffed softly.

"What's wrong?" Joan asked.

"I don't have feelings for you anymore," I said. She frowned.

"That wasn't—," she started. I shook my head.

"I know. For her, I mean. I thought I still wasn't over her. I am," I said. A weird, weird feeling. "I hated seeing you kiss Jack earlier too, I don't think I hate it anymore."

"That's good, right?" She asked.

"Yeah, very good."

"It might be because you've seen us together so much."

"Yeah, maybe. This is good, it's like therapy." She physically deflated a little bit.

"Yes, I'll need some of that too," she started and moved a bit. "How are we going to do this? Do you know what's next?"

"Not in the slightest."

"Let's get downstairs, then. It's good to know, though. Thank you for telling me."

I stood up, holding my hand out to help her up.

"They must miss us, I said I was gonna get you in a minute or so and we're, what, fifteen minutes later?"

"I think so," Joan replied. "But it's good to know anyway. Explains why you acted the way you did."

Foot by foot we shuffled through the hallway, past Thomas' blood. It looked fucking awful, it might get old to read but I could still see him laying there in the centre of it all.

"It does feel bizarre, everyone dying in one evening. Well, not everyone, luckily, but you understand what I'm saying."
"I think that's just the trauma," I replied.
"Ah. Lovely."
"Isn't it just?" We quickly walked around the corner. The long hallway with paintings stretched out in front of us.
"What made you buy these things?" I asked as we walked past some of the shit she gathered.
"The history behind them. Some of them I simply liked a lot. Do you not?"
"It's not really my style, but I can definitely respect it." They were still weird as hell.
"That's good," she replied.

We walked past the red curtains, now closed completely. I couldn't see downstairs anymore, we had to walk down the stairs to actually see the downstairs. I picked a rose from the pot and gave it to Joan. She tucked it behind her ear. It looked good on her.
"It looks good on you," I said. She smiled. We walked down the stairs, still as beautiful as before.

Joan's gaze went into my eyes and then behind me. Her face turned pale white and a loud scream came from her mouth. As if moved by her scream I turned around to see what the fuck was going on. I let out a scream just as loud, if not louder. There, high above the ground, hung Marilyn, golden rope wound around her neck, eyes closed. A rose in her black hair, just as Joan had.

"Oh god!" Joan yelled. I ran down the stairs, almost skipping every other step. Joan followed closely, though she wasn't as quick because of her heels. I didn't say a thing. I was so focused on getting down as quick as I could that I barely heard Jack and Scott come into the area.

"What the hell!" Jack yelled.

"Nobody touch anything!" Scott said.

"Get her down!" I yelled as I started yanking on one of the gold ropes, completely ignoring what Scott said. Surprisingly it worked, Marilyn floated down as I let the other gold rope get pulled into the air. Her limp body swayed on the movement.

"Is she still alive?" Joan asked. Scott got Marilyn to the ground and gently put her down. I couldn't move a muscle. It was like I was frozen, all I could do is look at it. Scott got rid of the golden rope around her neck and checked for pulse. He held for a couple of seconds, then opened one of her eyes. Bloodshot all throughout. A wave of tingles went down my spine, it looked gruesome. Her neck wasn't any better, bruised all over. There was no way she was still alive. My head knew that, but for some reason it didn't translate yet.

"She is gone," Scott said.

"No she isn't. You're not right," I said. Movement came back to my body like all I needed was a trigger and I kneeled down next to her and Scott.

"I am," Scott replied. I looked at him, then back at Marilyn. Thought after thought flooded my head. She couldn't be, she was here just a minute ago. She wasn't shot or poisoned, maybe she just needed a boost to get her heart back to beating.

"I can fix it," I murmured and started pushing down on her chest in rhythmic beats. I waited a second and breathed air into her. Her lips felt so much different from when she was still conscious, or you know, alive. Scott pulled me from her lips.

"She's no longer here, berratare," he said. I pushed his hand off of me.

"Don't touch me," I said and pushed on Marilyn's chest. Scott pulled me up from the ground and into the kitchen. I shot looks at jack and Joan but neither of them came after us. Good couple of friends I made here.

"Let go!" I said and tried to get the fuck out of his grip. Mate, he was stronger than I imagined him to be. "She'll die! Let me go, you bastard!" Scott pinned me up against a wall and even though I fought valiantly, I couldn't loosen his grip even a little bit. It was a little fucked up to be in a house with your superior self.

"Leo, calm yourself," he said. "This is not the moment to make a scene."

"I can save her!"

"No, you can not. Marilyn has passed away. Only god can save her now."

"Spare me the religious bullshit, Scott. She's not dead yet. Let me go!"

"She has passed away. I know you are aware of that."

"She's not," I said with an uncertain voice. Scott's hands were like meathooks. A couple minutes more and they would start breaking down my cells. Scott didn't reply.

"She's not. She can't be," I said. An uneasy feeling set into my stomach. "She was alive just a minute ago." My muscles turned into clay. Scott slowly loosened his grip and I just stood there, against the wall.

"Compose yourself, Leonardo. If not for yourself, do it for the others."

"Why?" I asked. "How do you do it?"

"Experience," he said.

Experience. He did. He had it. I didn't. The closest I came to a murder before I got sucked in here was through

194

writing. I haven't even really seen death before. Now Thomas and Marilyn were gone. The others too. Samuel, Nancy, the cunt. Sorry, count. Weird, weird, weird situations. I cared more about them than I thought, apparently. Thomas and I were doing so good, too. We got to know each other. We bonded, I'd even say. Marilyn and I, well, we hadn't gone that far. Far enough to care. We went pretty far emotionally. As did Thomas and I.

"However, keeping it all in during investigations and letting it out later does the trick."
"What?"
"Save the emotions for later. Not when the situation at hand requires a clear head."
"That's unhealthy," I said.
"It works. As of right now, you need something that works."
"I need to get the fuck out of here. That's what I need."
"You know I can not allow you to leave, Leonardo. I'm sorry about Marilyn, truly, but leaving would incriminate you severely."
"I don't care!"

I wasn't going to stay here forever anyway. Who fucking cared about Leonardo, handsome as he may be. I didn't. I had a life outside this bullshit. It wasn't much but at least there weren't any murders. Worst thing that happened to me was my girlfriend cheating on me. Who fucking cares. Who genuinely fucking cares. Fuck Jessica. Fuck Jason.

"You should. It would be detrimental to both your life and your business. Two things I assume you care for."
"Are you blackmailing me?"
"Dear god, Leonardo, no," he said, seemingly actually shocked that I got that vibe. "I'm looking out for you. Your

vision is admirable and having you here has been a great help."

I didn't say anything for a second. I *was* the Watson to his Sherlock. I closed my eyes. A little dry, probably hadn't drunk enough water. Watson needed to get some watser. God. The noise in my head was loud. I could still do it. Turn off my emotions. I didn't want to, it was hard to get back out. Once they're off, they're off for a while. Usually, at least. Haven't experienced as much death before. I opened my eyes and stared blankly at Scott for a moment.

"Are we alright?" He asked. I nodded.
"It's off," I just said. The thing was, it wasn't all gone. Not like it was usually. I still felt it. Kind of. I didn't hear my thoughts anymore. I just felt my brain getting tireder and my soul was filled with what I could only describe as white noise. Scott patted me on the shoulder and nodded towards the area he just pulled me away from.
"I don't want to see it, Scott. I don't know if I can keep it off if I do." Scott sighed, in a 'let me think real quick' type of way.
"Alright, if you deem it best. I'll tell you what I deduct." He walked off into the hallway. Fuck. I sat down on the ground and closed my eyes. Fuck.

Chapter 14

"… Discreetly, yeah?" Voices echoed into my ear.

"Yeah yeah yeah, settle down. No need to fuss. The lad's not gunna be traced back to anyone."

"Good, good. Now hurry away, Richie."

"Not so fast, I ain't doing this for nothin', am I?"

I tried to open my eyes, but it was like they were glued shut. My stomach hurt, I didn't know where I was. I tried reaching around but I didn't feel anything.

"Quiet now. You'll get your end when you have completed what you need to do." I heard grumbling, it came closer to where I was.

"Fine. But ya better come through, or the whole of London will know." Light flashed around me and I felt the area I was on start to move.

"Wait," I started. It didn't come out. Instead, there was a weird sound.

"Sssh," I heard and a cover was put over me. Fear spread through my body but I couldn't do shit.

"Nardo." I shivered and opened my eyes, looking around confused. Was I back home?

"Dozed off, have you?" Jack asked. Right. My name wasn't actually Nardo. I was still there. I rubbed my eyes and yawned.

"I guess I have, yeah. What's up?" I asked, trying to get rid of an uneasy feeling. Jack sat down next to me and was sort of anxiously looking around.

"I think Scott killed her," he whispered. I frowned.
"Who, Mari?" I whispered back. I didn't know why we were whispering, but Jack was obviously anxious so I automatically whispered along. Jack nodded.
"Yeah, Mari. I know you and Joan didn't do it and I didn't either. That leaves one guy."
"He was her date," I said.
"Yeah he was, but how long did they know each other?"
"I don't know, but why would he kill her?"
"He said she killed Thomas," he replied. I tried my best to look shocked. It was very watered down.
"What?" I said as if I hadn't seen him die.
"Yeah, right?" I shook my head and frowned, closed my eyes for a second and looked back at Jack, who was still looking around anxiously.
"But why would he kill her for that?" I asked.
"Look, I don't know, but he was the only one who coulda done it."
"Besides you," I said, sitting up a bit.
"I wouldn't kill her, Nardo. You know that."
"You didn't like her all that much."
"Not enough to *kill* her."
"Whatever, I don't know who did it. I don't think either of you killed her." Not fully true. Men have killed for less. I sighed. I didn't care. She was gone, there was nothing I could do about it.
"Even if I found who killed her, it wouldn't bring her back."
"No, but you can bring her peace," Jack whispered. I turned my head to face him.
"No. I'm not gonna kill anyone. What do you care about her peace anyway?" He pursed his lips and nodded.
"Fair enough. I'll give you that," he said. "But maybe it's who killed the others. I care about Sam's peace."

"Samuel was an accident, Marilyn obviously wasn't. Look at the way she was hung."

"After being strangled first."

"Exactly my point. You think Scott killed the others too?" I asked.

"The others who could've are dead."

"Yes, but most are accidents."

"We don't know that." True. I put my head against the wall.

"What do you want to do, then?"

"All I want is to stay alive. Figured I'd share to keep you alive too."

"I'm working together with him, how is that information going to keep me safe?"

"Don't," he said.

"Work together?" I asked. Jack nodded. "If you suspect him, why are you here and not with him?"

"I told you, to share it with you."

"Is that the best way to go about—," I started, being cut off by Scott who walked around the corner.

"Berratare," he said and nodded towards the tiny office. I looked back at Jack who almost invisible shook his head. I looked back at Scott and nodded slowly.

"Yeah, I'll be right in. Have to finish my conversation. You go ahead," I said. Scott's gaze flicked from me to Jack and back at me.

"Ofcourse," he said politely and walked into the office. The blinds clacked against the window when he closed the door.

"Don't go, mate," Jack said. I sighed and bit my lip, then patted his shoulder.

"See you later," I said and walked up to the door. The cold handle slid down my hand and opened the door. There he was, in his chair, waiting for me. Scott. For the first time in the evening, he looked sort of tense. In a nervous way.

"So," I started.

"Yes," he said and pointed to the other chair. The desk was put to the side, the two chairs were now alone in the middle of the room. "Please, have a seat." And I did. I sat down in the chair in the middle of the room. I saw him nervously fiddle his watch. "What is it?" I asked. "What did you find?" He licked his lips and looked away for a second, then back at me. "The cause of death was strangulation. Contrary to what it seemed like, not by the curtain holdbacks. This death was caused by manual strangulation." He waited for my response.

I didn't *know* what to say. I knew it was, I saw the way her neck looked. God, I could still see it even though I only saw it for a minute. Bruised, red, blue and purple. Eyes bloodshot. All throughout bloodshot. I rubbed my eyes and pinched the bridge of my nose. It didn't go away. I could see it even with my eyes closed. Not in my imagination, I saw it in flashes in the black of my eyelids. Like a fever dream. I opened my eyes again and blinked. I exhaled and looked at the ceiling. Flashes of red blood spreading across the floor. Good god. I inhaled quickly and held it for a second. I felt Scott's big hand on my shoulder, but somehow it made it worse. It made it worse. I couldn't see anything. Nothing but the flashes. My breath, I couldn't. I couldn't breathe.

I exhaled loudly and blew all the air out of my lungs until I couldn't blow any more than already was out.

I inhaled sharply. Flashes still going. Tight airways. Good god. Fuck.

Once again I exhaled long and deep and I kept going until I physically could not breathe any more and all air was gone. Scott's soothing voice spoke soft words but I couldn't hear what he said exactly. His hand rubbed my back with a little bit of pressure, not too much, not too little. I inhaled slowly, remembering from when I was younger, a class of yoga and relaxation and how it helps. My lungs filled and blew up and felt like they were at their peak, then let go all of it again in a long, long breath out.

"It's all right. You're all right. All will be fine. Keep breathing. You're doing a good job. Now keep it going," I heard Scott say in his soothing voice. I tensed my muscles and stretched them out. Slowly I started getting back my normal vision. Thank fuck.

"I'm okay," I managed to get out.

"You are. It's okay. You're okay." I rubbed my eyes again and steadied myself on the chair.

"I am," I said and exhaled shakily. What the fuck was that.

"We can talk about a different matter for a while until you've regained spirit," he offered. I shook my head.

"I'm fine, really. I know she's been strangled. I saw the marks on her neck."

"Indeed," he said. "You're certain you do not want to wait?" I just nodded. I had to shake that shit off. I had to stop getting so attached to people here. All it did was bring me whatever the fuck that was just now and new trauma, probably.

"Alright," he started. He waited a second to see if I was actually alright. I was holding up, but alright? Far from it, to be fair.

"We can rule out Joan as culprit since the hands were too big to be hers."

"So it had to be a guy," I said, trying to pick up where we left off.

"Yes, or a woman with larger hands. However, Joan is not one with that quality."

"Okay, so it was one of us. Jack, you or me."

"Yes, that is indeed my conclusion. All that rests us now is to figure out which one exactly."

"I was with Joan," I said.

"Indeed. However, I can not rule out that you and Joan worked together. She may not have done the act itself but she could very well have orchestrated it."

"Are you serious?" I asked.

"Do I think this is the case? No. But, it is a possibility. Possibilities need to be examined. Do you follow?" He asked.

"Yeah," I said. I did. Ofcourse he had to. He was a detective. It's not guesswork with those guys. It's facts and leads.

"We can't be certain of anything until we have looked at everything available," he said. As I was saying. Facts and leads.

"Jack was acting suspiciously," I started. Scott nodded. "Indeed, however we must not make any haste with our conclusions." Alright. Sure. I didn't mind. I straight up kind of liked Jack, so I didn't mind looking over things first.

"Yeah, sure," I said.

Walking closely after each other we left the side room. Side room with my side hoe. Main hoe now, actually. My old main one was dead. His was too. His and mine were the same one. Now we were each other's. Jack and Joan were sitting in the sitting area, away from Marilyn's body.

202

Good thing, smart thinking. I couldn't see her from here. We had to move her sooner or later though, she was going to smell eventually. Death is death.

"Hey," I said. Joan let out a soft sound, looking startled. "God, you scared me," she said.
"Hey, Nardo," Jack replied. Both of them were a little pale. Lack of sleep, likely. Combined with all the murders. I was probably a little pale too. Haven't looked in the mirror for a while.
"Hi, by the way," Joan said and rubbed the back of her neck. Jack reached over to a glass of alcohol and reached it over to me. The no drinking was no more. Why the fuck not.
"Thanks," I said. I brought it to my lips, but then kind of limply put it back down.

I plopped down on a chair and put my head in my hands. I didn't *feel* like drinking. All I wanted was to get out. I didn't want to keep this shit up. I didn't feel like being Leonardo anymore. You would almost forget your own name in shit like this. I wasn't Leonardo. I was Mike. Michael. Michael Davis. American writer. How long have I even been here? Hours on hours, there was no fucking end in sight. Was this my hell? Being stuck forever in this murder fest? I get attached, murder. I get close to someone, murder. Deadass, I was sort of waiting for the others to die too. If not now probably soon. I went with my hands through my hair and rested my face in them again.

"Are you good, mate?" I heard Jack ask.
"Yeah," I replied, but didn't look up.
"You feeling lightheaded?" He continued. I shook my head.

"No, I'm fine," I replied.

"I assume we all know the procedure by now," I heard Scott say. "Mister Donovan, please join me." Some shuffling around and clinking of a glass on a table and off they went.

"God, it's so horrible," Joan said. I just hummed. I didn't mind a bit of silence. Got a bit of a headache, actually. Still not giving my thoughts the space to roam free. It was the best for that moment, like Scott said. But it wasn't a nice feeling.

"I keep seeing her," Joan went on. I hummed.

"I do too. All of them." She was silent for a bit. Taken aback, it felt like. Maybe just thinking.

"Did you see Thomas?" She asked. I sat up slowly and looked at her for a second before I replied.

"Yeah," I said. She looked at me like she wasn't satisfied with that answer. "Well it wasn't pretty."

"Was it bad?" She asked. I just nodded. She rubbed the back of her neck and stretched it a little.

"You alright?" I asked. She frowned.

"Not really, my neck feels stiff." She stretched her neck by looking up and down a couple of times.

"That's rough," I said. I didn't really care.

"Yes, it doesn't feel good," she said.

"Did you lift too heavy?"

"No, I don't think so."

"Huh. Maybe we've just been awake for too long."

"Have we?" she asked, now stretching sideways. "How long has it been?"

"Too fucking long," I replied. Joan twitched. She wasn't looking too good.

"Hey, seriously, are you okay?" I asked.

"I don't know, I feel odd," she replied.

"Did you eat or drink anything weird?" I asked.

"Just a drink," she said. Another twitch. "Ah, that hurt." She rubbed the back of her neck as if she was trying to polish silver.

"Let me see," I said and walked over. She showed her neck but I didn't see anything. "What drink was it?" She pointed to a pink-ish drink next to Jack's glass.

"Did Jack give it to you?" I asked. She nodded. A bigger twitch this time, her head jerked back pretty hard.

"Jesus," I said and stopped her from hitting her head.

"Shit," Joan half cried. She grabbed my arm and looked straight ahead.

I knew what she was doing, it was what I did when I was fucked up beyond return and I was trying to focus my mind to be able to form a thought. I held her by her wrist and tried rubbing her back a bit. Not for long, I immediately noticed her pulse. Pretty damn fast. I put my hand to her heart to check better. Her pulse wasn't lying, her heart was beating crazy fast.

"Hey," I said to get her attention. She looked at me with big pupils.

"Nardo, I don't feel good," she said, slightly hiding her panic. I say slightly but I noticed.

"What are you feeling?"

"I'm really stiff, I feel really anxious," she replied.

"Okay, heightened awareness and something with your muscles or something. Where did that drink come from?"

"I don't know, I think the kitchen," she said and twitched so hard she knocked my hand into the couch. I could've been hearing shit but I could've sworn I heard a soft crack. In her back, not my hand. My hand was fine.

"Ow!" She cried. "Mike, make it stop!"

"I don't know what it is!" I said. "I don't know how to stop it!" I felt panic creep up on me. Was she next? I was *here*

205

for fucks sake. I couldn't *help her* and I was *here*. Why was I *here*? If I couldn't *fucking. Help.* What was the *use*?

Another twitch, making her slam her head into the couch. She was almost bending over, but through her spine. How the fuck did that happen? What fucking kind of shit did that? *Bending* through her *spine*. It was like that shit you see in horror movies when someone is possessed and they fucking bend through their spine. It was like her spine was curling up, but quickly, so her head was yanked the fuck back.

"Ah!" She yelled. I could barely hear it, it was like the air was smacked out of her.
"Scott!" I yelled.

The door swung open, Scott's face questioning. The questioning face soon turned into a concerned one as Joan twitched again. Each time looked even more painful than the one before.
"What do you know?" Scott asked me as he hurried to Joan.
"She drank a drink and she started having neck aches," I said. Jack ran out of the room as soon as he heard Joan's cries of pain.
"What's this?" He asked, face even more concerned than Scott.
"Are you still able to breathe normally?" Scott asked Joan. She nodded but didn't say anything. Face grimaced from pain.
"Hey, what is this?" Jack asked again.
"Can you open your mouth?" Scott asked Joan. She tried, but didn't get much farther than slightly opened. This made her panic even more.

"Has your neck been sore for long?" He asked. "Yes or no is enough." She shook her head.
"We could be right on time," Scott said. "That's good. Leo, was the first compulsion small?"
"Yeah, a little bit, yeah. But they got bigger fast."
"What the hell is going on?" Jack asked once more.
"Joan isn't doing too good," I said.

My heart was in my fucking anus. I felt hot, my brain did too. My brain was still sort of stuck on no feelings, but it was like you put your car in the wrong gear while trying to move. Having it in park while you're already trying to go fast. Your car will break the fuck down. A big, big twitch hit Joan and she fell down from the couch.

"Joan!" Jack yelled out. He was already by her side, looking more and more scared as the seconds passed. She didn't get back up, instead she kept arching back. Some of her other muscles started to twitch too, it was like she was having a seizure. Was she?
"Is it a seizure?" I asked.
"We need to get her to a safer space," Scott said. "Jack, get pillows and put them on the floor. We need to create a safe space for her. Leo, help him out."

Without hesitating I grabbed pillows. Jack seemed a bit in shock, not moving yet. I prodded him and threw the pillows on the floor. I saw Scott keeping her from hitting herself on the sharp table edges. It was even worse than before. She could barely make noise anymore, arching back more than before while her muscles were spasming. Jack came out of his shock — enough to get pillows, at least — and pillow after pillow filled the floor.

"Get her on!" I yelled at Scott as I ran to them. We picked her up. Her skin was boiling hot. Her eyes were the only thing I saw, full of panic and pupils wider than a fucking cocaine addict.

"It's gonna be okay," I said. We gently put her down, away from the sharp tables. With one last big twitch, her body relaxed and her cries filled the room. Jack threw himself down on his knees beside her and held her head in his hands.

"I'm here, darling, you'll be okay," he said, trying — but failing — to keep his voice from cracking. "I love you, I love you always." Joan couldn't do anything but cry loud cries. Jack stroked her hair and held her hand.

"I love you, Joan. I love you so much." Good fucking god. I felt a lump set into my throat.

"Is there anything we can do?" Jack asked, not looking away from Joan for a second.

"We don't have the right tools to treat her, we cannot do anything," Scott said. "I'm really, very sorry."

"What is it?" I asked.

"Undoubtedly strychnine poisoning." I didn't know that one. Didn't make me feel any better.

"How long does she have?" I asked.

"I can't say," Scott started, his voice a little unsteady. He coughed and composed himself. "It varies per case. It could be anywhere between minutes to hours. The convulsions will last a minute each and will be cut off by a period of around ten minutes of — if she's unfortunate enough, conscious — pain. Im really sorry, I am."

"Can we take her pain away?" Jack asked while stroking his wife's face.

"All we are capable of now is hoping she will lose consciousness sooner rather than later," Scott said.

"Please help me," Joan gasped in between cries. Her muscles slightly twitched.

"Joan, I love you, please," Jack cried.

"I love you," Joan managed to get out before her second convulsion started.

Further back and back went her head. Small gasps filled the air next to Jack's cries. Scott and I both could do nothing but watch. That was the worst part. We couldn't do shit. We couldn't do fucking shit beside *watching her* in her pain. I couldn't tear my eyes away. I didn't want to look. I couldn't look away. I couldn't look away from the woman I once though would be my wife one day, slowly dying. I wasn't there next to her. Jack was. I loved Jack too, just in a different way. He seemed emotionally in as much pain as his wife was physically. Thomas hadn't seen Nancy die. Jack was doing that very thing.

"Is there really nothing we can do?" I asked.

"Nothing besides making her as comfortable as possible and pray she will feel as little of it as possible," Scott said. I turned my head away from Joan. It felt like I was killing her myself, even though I wasn't doing anything. That was it, I wasn't doing anything. I wasn't helping her. I wasn't relieving her pain. I was looking at it like a sadistic motherfucker. Joan gasped and stopped moving again. She wasn't crying. She wasn't yelling. She was gasping for air like she couldn't breathe.

"Joan, Joan," Jack said. Joan couldn't say anything. Her jaw was a little bit forward and didn't seem to be able to move. She was just looking at the ceiling, eyes flicking furiously and quickly from Jack to the ceiling. Eyes mortified. She bonked on her chest and made eye signals to Jack. She couldn't breathe. She grasped at his face, his wet face. Tears streaming down.

"Joanie," he managed to get out. "I love you. You're the best thing that happened to me. I love you." With a last gasp Joan's eyes rolled back and closed slightly. Scott sniffed and rubbed his eyes for a second. Jack cried. I didn't know what to do. I didn't know what the fuck to do. I didn't know what I felt. Joan started arching again, this time no longer conscious. Arching further and further. Thank god she wasn't conscious anymore.

Soft cracks echoed through the room. Her muscles were spasming, making her look like she was having a seizure all while arching more and more back. I couldn't think. I didn't turn anything off this time. It was automatic. I couldn't form any thoughts. All I could do is look. All I saw was Jessica. Jessica dying right in front of my eyes. When I wished her to die a painful death after we broke up I didn't mean like this. I didn't want her to be in pain. Nothing was bad enough to deserve this.

I sat down next to Jack and put my arm around his shoulder. He hugged me, facing away from Joan, and cried. I softly stroked his back. His fingers drilled into my back, it was like he was holding onto me for dear life. Scott sat down in a chair and gripped the arm of it. Joan's body relaxed and she flopped over. Jack let go of me and scrambled to get a hold of her body. He clasped her hand and held it to his heart. He didn't say anything, he just sat there. Neither Marilyn nor Thomas compared to this one. It hit a little too close to home. I knew Jessica for years and years. I had the biggest bond with *her*, even though Joan technically wasn't her.

I dried my cheeks with toilet paper and tossed it in the bin. I placed my hands on the small sink and looked at myself. I looked like myself, still, but different. More like me from my real life. Red eyes from crying, hair fucked up. Dark under eye circles.

"Who the fuck are you?" I asked. It was stupid. It was cliche. I didn't care. I wanted to know who the fuck I was. Silly suit still on. The one I put on with Marilyn. Seemed like days ago already. It was barely hours.

I let my gaze blur. I *was* tired. I didn't know what time it was, but I knew it was closer to morning than it was to night. Crazy how much happened in the span of one night. That's what you get in a book. I'm never going to write again. All it did was fuck me up. If not by swallowing me, it was just by making me unhappier about my own life. I wasn't as inspired as before. I wasn't as young as before. I wasn't as happy as before. I was sad and old and now trapped in my own creation. What if I was next? I promised Joan not to let her die. But here we were. I stood by and watched. Another death. They seemed to get more gruesome as time went by. This one was poisoning, that's for sure. Strychnine, Scott said. I didn't research that one. I only needed two when I started out and one of those I didn't even know yet back then. In all fairness I didn't know the second one either, I researched the quinine for another book.

"You're a bitch," I said to my reflection. "Little fucking bitch." I opened the tap and let the water flow over my hands. I scooped some of it and splashed my face. Cold, the pipes must be freezing outside. I ran some through my hair and tried getting it back into some form of a shape. How was I supposed to get out? Out of this world, back into my own. Before I knew it I could be dead. Actually dead or story dead, no idea. Dead nonetheless. I splashed some water on the mirror. Small drops ran down it.

I stepped out of the bathroom, into the hallway. I pinched the bridge of my nose. The door to the small balcony was *right* in front of me. Should I? Only to see if he was still there. Maybe he *was* still alive. I shook my head even though it was fucking stupid. No one could see me. I turned my ass around and walked back to the sitting area. A bang shot through my ears and a chip of the wall fell down right past my head. I looked back for a split second out of reflex — not seeing anything, ofcourse, it was just a second — and ran around the corner as fast as I could, into the sitting room.

Chapter 15

My heart was pushing the blood through my head at an alarming rate. No one around, I was alone. That didn't stop me from running, fuck that shit. The shooter had legs, probably. He could run right after me. How was I so sure it was a guy you ask? All the women were dead. Speaking of which, the pillows were still on the ground. I didn't care in that moment. I cared more about getting the fuck away than about Jessica.

I ran through the kitchen, a couple of steps up the staff staircase and fell down. I pushed myself up and sat against the wall. Out of breath, completely destroyed. I was the worst pick for a horror movie, I'd die. Luckily this was a detective, I still had a chance. It SO barely missed my head. I grasped the railing and leaned my head against it. Still panting.

"What the fuck," I whispered. I rubbed my temple as if there was anything there. It was like phantom pain, I didn't have it but it felt so real that I had to check if there actually wasn't anything. There wasn't.
"Fuck," I said. You'd think being a writer would give me a bigger library of words to choose from. It didn't.
"Fuck," I said again. I aggressively rubbed my temple again. Not to check this time. I just had an issue wrapping my head around it. I almost died. Son of a fucking bitch. Couldn't I pause this story? I didn't want to be next. God damn it. Who the fuck did it?

"Who was that?" I heard, being yelled from wherever. I froze and held on to the railing for dear life. So tightly my knuckles went white.

"Anyone here?" I heard. Jack ran into the kitchen. He couldn't see me sitting behind the wall of the staircase. Not yet, at least. I quietly scooted a step upward. Maybe if I was really quiet I could make a run for it.

"Scott?" Jack asked as he ran through the kitchen. I scooted up another step. His dark brown head of hair came around the corner, followed by his green eyes and suit.

"Nardo, what was that?" He asked.

"I got shot at."

"What?" He asked.

"I got shot—," he interrupted me.

"No, I understood what you said," he said. "Where?"

"In the hallway."

"I'll be damned. Are you alright?" I stared at him for a bit. There were only two people still alive. Him and Scott.

"Did you do it," I stated. Didn't ask, I stated.

"No, are you insane? I don't even have a bloody gun."

"You could've asked Marilyn where hers was before you killed her," I said.

"Are you messing with me? Why would I do that?"

"Did you kill Joan?" That question seemed to hit him hard.

"Piss of Nardo," he just said and walked away.

"Jack, wait," I said, not too convincing. He didn't stop. "Jack."

"Don't move out of the way next time," he said without looking back. Chills ran down my back and my adrenaline changed directions. He fucking shot me. Doesn't matter if he missed or not. He tried to kill me.

"Dick," I yelled and charged at him without a moment of hesitation. He turned around right in time to get a fist to the cheek. He got sent a couple of steps back, touched his cheek and looked at me in disbelief. Then turned angry.

"Lowlife," he said.

"You stole her!" I yelled and went in for another punch. He blocked it.

"Who?" He asked.

"Joan!" He looked down confused for a second, then looked up with the angriest face he had yet.

"Joan," he said. "So I was right." Right? Did he think she cheated on him with me? Like he did to me? Was that why he killed her? Fucking pretentious dick. I didn't kill *them*.

"Fuck you!" I yelled and went in for a rib punch.

He blocked it and somehow turned me around and kicked me in the ass, making me stumble steps away from him. I didn't fall, but it was way too fucking close. This guy kicked my ass in the most literal sense. I turned around, face even angrier than his was before. Like anyone would, come on. Imagine you got kicked in the ass. Most humbling thing.

"I knew it!," he yelled. "You're a pathetic little man!" Look who was talking.

"No, *you're* pathetic," I spit and swung my left arm a little so he blocked that side and then struck the same cheek I had before again. He coughed. I got some tricks too.

"At least I'm original," he said and punched me right in the face.

The motherfucker thought he was slick. He did get me pretty good, though. The echo of his punch rang through my head. I blinked my eyes a couple times and shook my head. Blood dripped down on the floor. I stepped in it, by accident, and left prints of it every step I took. I didn't know where it was from, my nose didn't feel like it bled. It did hurt but no blood as far as I could tell. I wiped my mouth. Bloodied hand. Ah.

"Why did you do it?" He yelled.
"You did it first," I said, lips numb from the hit. He hit again, my side of the head this time. I stumbled to the side. Jesus fuck, I didn't think I was *this* out of shape. "You're mental," he said and walked after me.

He kicked me in the back before I could catch my breath, knocking the air the fuck outta me. I gasped and fell down against a table. Couldn't do it with a gun but I had no doubt he could fucking kill me with his hands. I looked back at him and sat up a little bit. Another hit, I blocked it just enough and right after hit him with a left hook. He took a step back and scoffed, then returned the favour with a hook to the jaw. I tried for a knee in the good ole nuts but he dodged it. I could barely see his face. The shape that was Jack came closer.
"Don't fight battles you can't win, bastard," he said and hit me right on the temple.

I blinked and tried getting my head up. It was like I was drunk as a goose, eyes rolling around to find a point of focus while wobbling my head around. Where was Jack? I squinted and slowly sat up. A hit of pain shot through my upper body and head but I managed to stay up.
"Fuck," I said. A shape came into my sight. I got scared, like one does, and reflexively threw a punch. It got blocked softly.
"Leo," Scott said. "It's alright. It's Scott. You lost consciousness but you're alright." His warm hand held my back so I didn't immediately fell back over. That son of a bitch knocked me out.
"Where's Jack?" I asked.

"He is currently detained. There's no longer a need for fear. I am terribly sorry I couldn't tear him from you sooner."

"Tear him from me?" I asked. Scott hesitated and licked his lips, then pressed them down on each other slightly. "He was in the process of creating his next murder," he said.

"Jesus, he was? How bad is it?"

"You will live," he said. I frowned.

"Well goody me, thank god," I replied sarcastically. "Where is Jack?"

"In the wine cellar. I could not think of a better place to keep him until authorities arrive."

"Huh," I said. Must be drunk by now then. Depending on how long I was out. "Thank you, Scott. For getting him away."

"It's my duty," he replied.

"Right, but thanks anyway." He smiled. Cute smile.

"I must say, it would be terribly lonely to investigate without you."

"We're the only ones that survived, not much else to investigate," I said.

"On the contrary. This opens up a new world of questions — and answers alike."

"Can I talk to him?" I asked.

"If you feel up to facing him I suppose we could visit the cellar for a moment."

The hallway was slightly dark, darker than it was before at least. I had to make a conscious effort not to suck on my bloodied lips. The cuts in it weren't deep but I knew they would probably open up if I would suck on them. That's where most of my mind was for the time we walked. Don't let authors fool you with nice inner dialogue after fights, most that went through my head was pain and trying to ignore it. I did notice it was darker than before. It was obvious. The lights were dimmed. Those in the whole house were. They were like that when I woke back up. The banging on metal was even clearer.

"Can he hear me?" I asked.

"Perhaps, if you speak loudly." The banging didn't stop.

"Let me out!" I heard sort of softly. Muffled by the door. He wasn't whispering.

"Jack!" I said. The banging stopped.

"Nardo, help!" I heard in return.

"Why did you do it?" I yelled.

"I didn't do nothing!" He yelled back.

"Son of a bitch! Why?"

"Nardo, let me out!"

"Like hell I will!"

"Watch your back!" The guy was down there making threats.

"Can he still?" I asked, looking back at Scott.

"Doubtful. There is no poison present, neither can he do any physical harm."

"Why did you kill them?" I yelled at the big door.

"Nardo, I swear, I didn't!" He yelled. Trying to get me to believe him even though he almost killed me. Why the fuck would he think I would defend him to the police when he tried to kill me *twice*?

"Get me out!" He yelled. I turned to Scott again.

"Did you lock both doors?" I asked. He nodded.

"Secured until the authorities arrive."

"How comfortable is he down there?" I asked.

"Fairly. There's a chair, bread and water and the lights are turned on."

"Why did you do that?"

"Every person has to be able to drink or eat."

218

"No lights then," I said. I pointed to the switches next to the door.

"Which one?" I asked.

"The bottom one," he said. I pushed it. A buzz sounded and just a second after Jack screamed.

"Bastard! You get me out! Right now!" He yelled.

"That's quite enough," Scott said and gestured me to walk back to the hallway.

"Don't leave me here!" Jack yelled.

"What, scared?" I asked.

"Nardo, please, don't leave me here!" He yelled. Scott led me away. Jack started banging on the metal door again.

"Nardo!" I heard before we closed the door to the hallway behind us.

Scott and I quietly sat down on one of the couches. Turns out I *was* right before. It *was* the rich asshole. I should trust my first instincts more often. Why did I let myself get close to him? It was Jason. Different name, same asshole. I closed my eyes for a second to get rid of the headache. Didn't go away. I opened my eyes again.

"What do we do now?" I asked.

"Now we wait," Scott said. I sighed. For how long? When was I gonna get back to my own world? The mystery was solved.

"How *did* he do it?" I asked.

"Accomplish the murders?" Scott asked. I nodded.

"Going from what I've gathered, he must have poured the poison into sir Stonier's glass when he went to the bathroom. No one suspected it. He discarded it in sir Stonier's office, leading to mister Singretti's death. He used strangulation to kill Marilyn when I was studying my finds and you were with the lady Donovan upstairs. He

219

must have slipped poison into the lady Donovan's drink when we were going over our finds."

"And Nancy and Thomas were through Marilyn, both kind of indirectly. Right?"

"Indeed." Then why was I still here? I solved the mystery.

"Either way, I am grateful to have had your help. There is no doubt in my mind that I would have missed several leads if it weren't for you. So, thank you. Genuinely."

"Of course. Glad I could help. Sorry about your girl," I replied.

"Thank you. I must admit, it's better to find out about her capability to murder now rather than later."

Yeah, I bet. I still felt guilty about my part in Thomas' murder, though. What was I even talking about. It happened just hours ago. 'Still' guilty. I looked around the room. Still the same one I came into the story in.

"Do we really just wait?" I asked.

"We do, yes. What else do you propose?"

"I don't know, there must be something." Do stories usually just cut here? Maybe. I've never been in a story before. Do we really just sit around at the end of the story? Why was I still here? Did I need to act as witness? Couldn't the real Leonardo do that? I felt a little restless. Maybe it was all the shit that happened. Who knew. I've never witnessed as much death either so who fucking knew. New trauma will do that to you. Maybe. I didn't know.

"Is there something we missed?" I asked. I couldn't shake that feeling. Like I left home without my keys or some shit.

"We can take a look at my work if that would soothe your nerves," Scott said.

"Yeah, maybe," I replied.

Scott opened the door of his side room office. The click clacking of the blinds felt nice and familiar. His desk was full of notes and even some drawings. I recognized the gun Marilyn shot with. It was just a little bit different. He probably drew it as reference of what to look for. He knew the bullet, after all. He had a drawing of it. I saw a drawing of some pills and vials with names underneath them. His handwriting was pretty nice. Better than mine.

"Do you have a report or something like that?"
"Not yet, I will write one tomorrow. I need to get some rest and a clear head before I do. I cannot make any hasted conclusions."
"Smart," I said. Too bad though, would help me figure out what the fuck all of this was. To connect it, I mean. This was a whole bunch of loose papers. I was feeling a little sleep deprived too, my brain didn't function like usually. I shuffled through some papers, barely registering what was on it. What was I even looking for? It was pretty clear Jack did it. I got first hand prove of that. Maybe that's why I was still here. To testify against Jack as surviving victim. Why the fuck did *I* need to do that though. Again, couldn't real Leonardo do that? If there was one.

"Do you have anything to add to it?"
"I don't know what you already know. The count was the reason Jack's father killed himself. Did you know that?"
"I didn't. That is excellent work, Leo." He took a notepad and started scribbling on it.
"Thanks," I said. Was *this* my purpose, then? Helping Scott?
"Did Jack have Marilyn's gun?" I asked. Scott stopped scribbling.

221

"Yes, he did," he said.

"How did he find it?"

"He told me he had stumbled upon it. I do not think he told me the truth but he did find it."

"Where is it now?"

"I have put it with the other evidence."

"Huh."

"I heard a shot. Was it aimed at you?" He asked. I nodded.

"I'm terribly sorry. I should have been there."

"No, that's okay. I get it. You can't be everywhere." He nodded and started scribbling again.

"Where were you, though?"

"Gathering evidence of Marilyn's death."

"On the balcony?" At the end of the hallway I was shot at?

"No, in the main hallway." I would've seen him when I ran through the sitting area.

"Where?"

"By the stairs."

"Oh, alright," I said.

My heart beat faster. I rummaged through some more papers but it wasn't very effective. My hands were shaking. What if Scott? What if *he* did it? Why the fuck would he shoot me? Jack tried to kill me *later,* but did he actually? He just knocked me out. For all I knew he just left me there. I looked at Scott with a side eye. Didn't turn my head. Still scribbling away. Jack *and* Scott were downstairs when Marilyn died. He was with Joan right after Marilyn's murder when Jack went to warn me. About Scott. I didn't know about strychnine but it could just as well be a poison that set in later. Ideal for framing Jack. You know, the one that was convinced Scott killed people. The threat. I wasn't even here yet when the count died so who knows what he did.

"Are you alright, Leo?" Scott asked.

"Hm?" I asked.

"Can you find everything alright?"

"Yeah, there's some interesting things here," I replied. I needed to get away. Whether he did it or not. Why would I risk my life?

"Though I do need to pee. I'll be back in a second," I said.

"Of course," Scott said. I calmly walked out of the office, acting as normal as I could.

Was I imagining things? Why *would* Scott kill anyone? He didn't even know any of these people before. He knew most about poisons out of everyone, though. He knew plenty of methods to kill. I hurried to the bathroom, through the slightly dark house. Why did he turn the lights down? It was spooky enough as it was. Why would he take me onto his investigating if he was the killer? That would be stupid as hell.

I pulled the bathroom door closed behind me and sank down on the toilet. Mind racing as always. If Scott did it, why did he lock Jack in the cellar? He couldn't keep him there forever to starve him. He couldn't do anything to him there. Maybe it was just to help me believe jack did it so I would help blame him instead of Scott. That would actually be smart. I did actually need to piss now. I put up the toilet seat and undid my belt. Reminded me of Marilyn. Everything here reminded me of *someone*. This toilet reminded me of Nancy, since she died on it. Mindlessly I started pissing. Man's gotta do what a man's gotta do. I sighed. What was this man gonna do though. Maybe check to see what Jack has to say. Scott locked both doors, opening just one wouldn't hurt. I fastened my belt again and flushed the toilet.

Quietly I stepped through the hallway. I could do that now, walk quietly. Thanks to these shoes. Scott wouldn't hear a thing. I stopped and shivered. No noise. Scott's footsteps made no noise. Jack's did. I didn't hear footsteps when I was shot. Fuck. I opened the door to the room with the cellar. No banging anymore. He probably got tired, maybe his hands started hurting. Gotta remember that he punched my face with them before too, must hurt at least a little bit.

"Jack?" I said after closing the door behind me. I walked up to the cellar door. No response. Maybe he was pissed off. I would be. If I got caught murdering. I would be even more pissed if I got locked up when I wasn't even the murderer.
"Jack, I'm gonna open the door," I said. I pulled the lock up and swung the door open. First thing I saw was red. The steps were filled to the brim with wine. A carpet of wine stretched out in front of me. Everything was filled. The iron door was completely underneath it. Imagine the cellar itself.

"Fuck, Jack!" I yelled. There was no way he was still alive. I dove down into the wine, tried opening my eyes to see but immediately regretted it. Closed them as fast as I could and went back up. There was no way to even see. There I was, waist-high in the wine. Jack was dead. I couldn't even see him. I knew the ceiling of the cellar was just slightly higher than the door. Less high than the top of the stairs, that was for sure. He drowned. Jack drowned. Jack drowned in the rosé. The switch in the wall, did I do this? Did I make all the wine in the huge basins in the wall fill the cellar?

"You sick son of a bitch!" I said, walking into Scott's office. "It was you *all this time.* How the hell did I not see anything?" Scott turned around confused.

"You killed them. *You* did. You sick motherfucker. You killed them. You pretentious fuck!" I said.

"What are you talking about?" He asked.

"You drowned Jack. You tried to shoot me!"

"I did no such thing," he replied.

"Cut the bullshit, I saw. You piece of shit. Why the fuck did you kill them?" He leaned back in his chair.

"You had to check, didn't you." He stood up from his chair and whipped out a gun faster than I could blink. He shot me right in the tit. Right lung. Never felt anything so painful. I slouched down against the wall. He crouched down next to me and sighed.

"You killed them," I spluttered.

"I did no such thing. However, *you* did."

"What?"

"After I caught you, I had no choice but to shoot you out of self defense. Unfortunately at that point I was too late, you've already done what you came here to do." He smiled a quick, fake smile. I coughed. Some blood came up. Good god. He shot me. He killed them all.

"Why?" I asked.

"I don't believe I owe you anything, friend," he said. "But, alas, for the sake of our short-lived partnership. I'm his son. Remember that cufflink? It did not belong to our good pal Sam. I am SS."

I couldn't say anything. I felt blood coming in every time I breathed. Drowning in my own blood. I knew what it was. He shot my lung. Soon I wouldn't be able to breathe anything but blood. I felt some drip down my nose and mouth. The panic was spreading even faster than the blood. I tried to control it, I knew the faster I'd breathe the faster I'd die.

"He abandoned me as a kid. I was his '*bastard*'. His dirty little secret," he said. "He didn't want me screwing up his reputation, so he dumped me like an old rag. He didn't care about me. He destroyed my life." That explained the dream I had. I spluttered some blood in an attempt to speak.
"My mother?" He asked. I nodded-ish.
"Mary Donovan." Jack's mom. I laid down my head. I couldn't keep it up. Scott must've been the one time Jack's mom cheated. He was Jack's brother. He just killed his own brother. And father. And — hold on. Marilyn was his sister. I frowned at him. He fucked his sister. And I thought Thomas fucking his niece was bad. What the fuck.

"Marvelous job. I was hoping you wouldn't, I actually came to like you. But, as they say, que sera, sera," he said. I coughed, more blood came along. I slowly breathed in again. A rush of blood came in. Barely any air. I tried grabbing something, anything, but there was nothing. My chest couldn't expand anymore, there was nothing to expand it with. Blood dripped down my mouth. Fuck. Scott became hazy, I couldn't breathe, I couldn't see, I couldn't do anything. I tried hitting him one last time but he stepped away with just a bit too much ease.
"Goodbye, Leonardo," he said.

Chapter 16

I gasped and moved all the body parts I could. The pain moved from my chest to my head. I heard a loud meow. "Fuck," I said and grabbed my head. A loud thumping went through it. Like it was beat with a jack-hammer.

"Son of a bitch," I said and sat up.

I opened my eyes, but couldn't pinpoint one specific thing. Almost like I was drunk. Maybe I just hit my head. I crawled up and leaned on a couch. It didn't feel very nice. Felt old and pretty rough. I plopped down in it and held my head in between my legs. The thumping became louder. Of course, more blood to it. I sat up again. Something went up to my leg. I jumped and screamed.

"What the fuck!" I yelled, followed by a stinging pain in my head. I tried focusing my eyes, wobbling on my legs. A cat. It was a cat. I looked around. A red lamp, a desk. A fallen chair. I scoffed a happy scoff.

"I'm back," I said. I plopped down on the couch again. "I'm back!" A wave of relief came over me. I was drunk as a motherfucker, but I was back. I was fucking back.

"Dude, you won't believe what happened," I said as I stroked my cat who walked by. He hissed at me.

"Jesus, I missed you too." I grabbed him and put him down on my lap. He immediately leapt off.

"Fine. At least you didn't eat me when I was out." I grabbed my phone.

"Jesus, only an hour later," I mumbled. "No wonder you didn't eat me. Wasn't hungry." I rubbed my head. It wasn't that bad. I didn't even fall on anything sharp. I *just* missed it. Must've imagined it, then. Real fucking weird. You'd think I'd be used to weird things by that point.

"Thanks anyway, though. I won't eat you either." I stood up, trying to find my balance. I wasn't hurt that badly but I was still really fucking drunk. I looked around me, again trying to find a point to focus my gaze on. It was dark in my room, only light came from my laptop. I stumbled towards it. Would it have the story? Would this be one of those things where authors get possessed and write a good fucking story? Or, in my case, a story at all.

I put the chair back up and carefully sat down in it. I could tell how stupid I looked doing it. I was drunk, not unaware. I squinted at my laptop and scrolled down to the end. Nothing. Samuel and Scott were working together. It was still my old story. I could just kill Scott off. No more murders. Though, to be fair, Samuel wasn't dead yet and neither was anyone else. This story was worse, though. It wasn't what really happened. If I just killed Scott, no one would know he even did it in the first place. I selected all the text from the end until I arrived in it. Should I? Should I really delete it? I bit my lips. No wounds on them anymore. Thank god. With one hit I deleted it all. The least I could do is *tell the story*. The real one. Not whatever the fuck the old one was.

Two knocks on my door. I turned around, startled.
"Who's there?" I asked.
"It's me, buddy. Open up for a second," I heard. It was a little muffled since it was through the door, but I was pretty sure I recognized that voice. I slowly stood up, almost sneaking to the door. My cat whirled around my legs while I sneaked on. I slowly opened the door, but only

a little bit. I stuck my head around the corner. There he was. I opened my door completely.

"Jack," I said with a smile. It was good to see him. He frowned.

"Jack?" He asked. I blinked and stared at him for a second. Right. Was I still drunk? I could see clearly again. Probably wasn't drunk anymore. It's been hours. I already got through most of the story.

"Sorry, Jason. What's up?" He looked a little uncomfortable.

"Jess wanted me to check up, she was worried about you. You all good?"

"Why didn't she come?" I asked.

"She didn't think you wanted to see her."

"And she thought you I *would*?"

"Alright, mate, I didn't want to come here either. Are you good? Just say yes and I'll be out of your hair."

It was weird to see him in his normal clothes. Alive, at that. Not beating me up. Though, to be very honest, I now understood why he got so mad. I sighed and looked down. Maybe this guy wasn't bad either. He went all the way here just to check.

"Wanna come in?" I asked.

"I'd rather not," he said. "No offense to you, but I know we don't like each other."

"Maybe. I don't blame you for Jess anymore. She and I never really were compatible," I said. He hesitated.

"Look, mate. I *am* sorry for the way things happened. Shouldn't have done it behind your back. But you can drop it, I know you're not keen on me."

"I saw you as the other guy, not as Jason. Sorry I called your dick tiny." He scoffed and grinned.

229

"Don't worry about it." He acted like Jack. Bet he could punch me the same way too.

"Hey man, I gotta finish a book, but do you want to get a beer sometime?" He looked as shocked as I was.

"Yeah, I guess," he said. I nodded.

"Nice. Can I get your number?"

"Uh, yeah," he scrambled through his pockets, with a slightly confused face. "Sure." He gave me his phone.

"Call yourself with it."

I plopped back onto my desk chair and continued writing. I felt lighter. Both from sobering up and facing Jack. I should've done both a long time ago.

'I shuffled sideways through the hall, trying to look anywhere but the red black hole that somehow sucked my gaze into it.
"Joan?" I said. I closed my eyes. Relying fully on touch I shuffled on, bump on the wall after bump.'

It was weird to write. I was there. I did all of that. Before I never even really wrote in first person. Now I was that first person. I remembered everything more clearly than I remember my own life. Don't know what the hell it was. Maybe I had a bad alcohol run, maybe I was so juiced out that I started having an awful vivid dream. Maybe it was because I hit my head — though less hard than I first thought. I don't know. Still do not know.

'Scott became hazy, I couldn't breathe, I couldn't see, I couldn't do anything. I tried hitting him one last time but he stepped away with just a bit too much ease.
"Bye, Leonardo," he said.'

I grinned and clicked save. It was a weird story, but it was mine. It was quite literally mine. 'Saved', it said. I closed the laptop, put it in a bag and put on my shoes. I went into the bathroom, considerably less nice than the one in the count's house, and ruffled my hair until it was decent. I wiped my face and stroked my t-shirt. Nice. Awful, but nice. After this shit was done I was gonna improve. No more alcohol. Not as much, at least. I grabbed the bag and then the doorknob. My cat screamed at me.

"What? What is it?" I asked. He went into the kitchen, tail up and ass out. "You want food? Is that it?" I asked. I sighed.

"You're in the way of fate, dude," I said. "I gotta get this book out there." I walked after him anyway.

The streets weren't as empty as the day before. It was pretty much the same time, just a different day. Leaves rustling underneath my feet. Walking, again. On the healthy grind. I even drank some water before I left. Cars drove by. I could've been one of them, but I wasn't. I was walking. Suckers. A frightening amount of them were TTJ cars, Jason's brand. They took off in this area. They did in the other parts of the world too, but this was the part it was almost every other car. Renewable and eco friendly energy. Good for him. It wasn't far to my publisher's office, luckily. Still wasn't great with cardio. Walking along the edge of prospect park, again. Right about where I saw Jessica and Jason yesterday. I passed it today. Neither of them were there.

I swung open the door with a smile. I did it. I finished it. I wrote my book.

"Hello mister Davis," the lady at the front desk said. Her name was Fleur, I believe.

"Hello, love," I said.

"Do you have an appointment?"

"No, I don't. Is he here?" I asked as I walked up to her.

"Sadly no, he isn't. Can I take a message?"

"Is there someone else here?"

"None of the people that work closely with you, unfortunately."

"Anyone else? Really, anyone will do," She checked her screen.

"We do have miss Michelle Damon," she said. "She's available for another hour."

"Fine, her then."

"Room 2.17," she said.

"Thank you," I said and took the stairs.

The halls were warm and inviting. The sun shone through the windows and made little flecks of sunlight dance through the trees onto the floors and walls. Thank god I was back. 2.13, 2.15, 2.17. I knocked on the door. "Come in," I heard. A woman's voice. Vaguely familiar. Maybe I *did* meet her before. I've been with this publicist for over ten years. I opened the door. I was a little nervous, for some reason. I felt the nerves crawl around in my stomach.

"Hey, I'm Mike," I said before looking in.

"Nice to meet you, Mike. I'm—," Marilyn.

It was Marilyn. I stopped in my tracks. Alive and beautiful as ever. Black turtleneck, jeans. Cute glasses on. Never before did I feel so giddy. My brain probably just used her face in my subconsciousness when I fell, but man did I feel lucky.

"Michelle," she continued.

"Hi," I uttered. Her beautiful blue eyes, I didn't think I would ever see them again.

"So, what do you have for me today?" She asked and pointed to a chair. I slowly started moving again. I couldn't look away.

"Ah, ehm, i finished a book," I said and sat down. She nodded and checked her screen. Scrolled up and down a little bit, then looked back. I hadn't looked away for a second. It was like I was hypnotized.

"Do you have it with you?" She asked. I nodded and put the laptop on her desk. She opened it with her beautiful fingers and looked at it for a second.

"Would you like some coffee?" She asked.

"Yeah," I said. "I would."

We spent the next two hours reading and sipping our coffees. She cancelled her original appointment to finish the story. She asked questions throughout, good ones. It was nice to see her again. Even if she wasn't really Marilyn. Jason wasn't really Jack either, but it was as close as it would ever get. I was glad the guy I was actually here for wasn't here. I wouldn't have met Michelle. Maybe I did base Marilyn off of her, subconsciously. Maybe I saw her in a hallway in this building some time ago. Who knows.

Most of the time she was silent, reading my story. I didn't once interrupt her if she didn't ask or say something herself. Half the time I wasn't even reading along, I was just looking at her. Not in a weird way, I just couldn't believe she was here. Alive, real. The time flew by quicker than any of the hours I spent inside the story. She looked very concentrated on it, her eyes flicked from page to page until finally she finished.

"So, he could pick any fake last name and he still chose 'Chase'?" She concluded. I laughed.

"He did. He's a man of theatrics," I said. She smiled.

"It was a very good story, Mike," she said.

"Thank you," I replied. Glad she liked her own story.

"I can't say officially yet because I do have to run it by the guys that work with you more regularly, but I think it's ready to be published."

"That's great news!" I said. "Thank you!"

"Of course," she said. "I'm happy you let me read it." I hesitated for a second.

"Yeah, of course. Thank you for reading it." She smiled. God, I didn't think I'd see that smile again.

"I'll send a statement over to them and I'll ask them to get in touch, is there anything else you need?" She asked.

"No, no, that's it. This is great," I replied.

"Well, if that's all, I think I'll get my break now," she said. I stood up.

"Thank you, really. Have a nice break." She stood up after me and led me out of her office. I waited at the door and turned back to her.

"Is there a chance I'll see you again?" I asked. I felt almost guilty for asking. I knew she wasn't with Scott anymore. Even if she was, Scott wasn't the best guy. Still. She smiled.

"If you want there to be," she said. I laughed.

"I do."

"Well, when do you want to see me again?" She asked. I grinned.

"When do you finish work tomorrow?" I asked.

"6.30," she said.

"7 tomorrow, then," I said.

"See you then," she said.

"See you then," I said.

I walked out of the building, closing the door behind me, with the biggest grin on my face I've had in a long time. I got a date. I got a date with Michelle. I was grateful I got sucked into the story, even if it still gave me fucking chills even thinking about it. God, life was good.

"Good day," I said to an older guy walking up to the building. He didn't reply, but I still felt really good. I shook my head and looked around me in awe. I laughed and started walking.

"Thank you, god," I said.

I rustled through my pocket and got my phone. The missed call from Jason was still in there. Missed on purpose, it was just to get his number. It was a surreal thing to see. I dialed the guy's number. Even though he wasn't in the office today, he'd probably still pick up. I knew him in and out. The phone rang a few times, but then got picked up, as expected.

"Mike?" I heard.

"Hey man, how are you?"

"Kind of in the middle of something, actually. What's up."

"Ah sorry, I'll make it quick. Guess what."

"That's not quick. Just say it," he said. I rolled my eyes. "I could *hear* that eyeroll, mike."

"Yeah yeah, I know you could, Stanley."

"So?"

"I wrote."